A SECRET WORTH KEEPING

DREW STRICKLAND

WWW.DREWSTRICKLANDBOOKS.COM

For Calypso,
The pot-jumper, the covered in dirt kitty, the stubborn girl,
the needy girl, the nurse cat, the caretaker, the family cat.

Thank you for loving us.

See you in the next one, my girl.

PROLOGUE

One headlight of the car still worked, illuminating the smoke rising from the hood of the car. What little of the hood there was left, anyway. Most of it was demolished and contorted, wrapping around the tree that the car had rammed into.

The horn blared with no hint of ending any time soon. Every single window was shattered, scattering glass all over the dirt, mixing with the mess of pine needles on top. The windshield was blown out from a huge hole in the center, the edges still clinging to the frame of the car.

The airbag inside the vehicle was blown out of the steering wheel, another one puffed up and now deflated in the passenger seat. The smell in the air was a mixture of exhaust, burnt rubber, and a tinge of copper.

Inside the vehicle, a woman stirred in the driver's seat. Her head lifted up slowly from the airbag, half of her face covered in talcum powder, the other half in a red rash from where the airbag had rubbed her skin raw. Her eyes were wide open, and if anyone saw, they would swear that she never blinked. Not even once.

She opened her door and stumbled out, falling onto the broken glass and pine needles on the ground. Her arms were scraped. One of her arms wasn't working too well, slumping to the side. Her entire body had shifted from her collarbone being broken.

But she was in too much shock to feel any of it.

The road up at the top of the hill curved around to the left, but at the bend, a fresh pathway led down to the wrecked car where the tires had dug tracks in the dirt. No skid marks touched the asphalt of the road, and if anyone were to drive the curve of the road, they'd never know anything was off unless they looked down the hill to see the car. The lack of streetlights made it nearly impossible to see anything in the night.

Luckily, a car pulled off to the side of the road, the headlights shining down at the accident. An older man stepped out of the driver's side door, his eyes wide from having witnessed the accident.

"Oh my god," he whispered. "Stay there, I'm coming down to you!"

Wasting no time, he worked his way down as safely as he could, the grade of the hill being a little steep. His knees hadn't had this type of strain in a long while.

The woman climbed to her feet and walked toward the man. Her hair was a mess, littered with tiny shards of glass and talcum powder. "Aaron!" she called out, as if she hadn't heard the man.

"Honey, you need to sit down," the man said, reaching her. "You've just been in a car accident."

The woman shook her head, finally hearing him. "I need to find my boyfriend. Have you seen him?"

The man looked behind her and didn't see anyone there. "Are you sure he was with you?" he asked, knowing that someone in shock might not realize where they are or where they were before getting into an accident.

"Aaron!" she yelled again. This time, she turned around and stumbled toward the car.

"Miss, please," the old man said, trying to keep up with her. "You look like you've been hurt." Her one arm no longer moved, and he could see what looked like a piece of bone sticking out near her shoulder, the blood smeared over her skin.

The woman didn't listen. Instead, she kept pushing on. The old man did his best to get in front of her, and when he did, that's when they both saw it.

"Oh my god," the man gasped.

Her boyfriend lay on the ground, a crumpled mess, against a tree that was about ten feet from the car. He had been ejected from the vehicle, missing the tree that the car had plunged into and finding another one. His neck was twisted in a way that neither of them had seen before, his legs pointing in different directions. His arm was wrapped around his body, almost looking like it was made of rubber.

"Aaron!" she screamed, taking two steps before falling to the ground and finally passing out.

ONE

Stella
Present Day

The black, wood-paneled cabin comes into view, and all I can worry about is what he's going to think. I steal a glance to my left, where Joel sits in the driver's seat, and try to get a read on him. His brow is furrowed, his lips a straight line across his face. So far, I've got no idea what's going through his head, but from the way he isn't expressing anything to me, I begin to worry it's nothing good.

The cabin looks a lot more modern than what most people would expect when they're told "cabin in the woods". It's not even so much the black that I think is giving Joel pause, but the turquoise color that lines the trim around the roof, highlights the window pop-outs, and completely washes over the door. This is no rustic spot, that's for sure.

But then again, Joel never gave me specifics. Never had any expectations. In fact, it was my suggestion that we go somewhere. I told him about a secluded little neighborhood up in the mountains where we could break away from our regular lives, and he was all for it. He just had to find time off of work, of course. My work schedule, however, is almost nonexistent, even though I'm a traveling nurse. But part of the reason for it being nonexistent isn't just because I keep my own hours, but because my clients are few and far between.

That's something I don't mention to Joel, of course. We've been seeing each other for about a month. We're still in the exciting part of the relationship. The one where we can hardly go an hour without texting each other, can't stop thinking of each other, and most of all, want to do nothing other than put our hands on each other's bodies.

Infatuated. That's probably the best description of what we are, although it comes off as almost stalker-like. I know I'm no stalker, and as far as I can tell, Joel isn't, either. I'm sure I'd be able to tell if he were. Plus, he wouldn't have given me the cash when I told him how much it was to book the cabin. I tried to protest, saying it was no problem for me to pay, but, well, that was a lie. The whole no-clients thing really puts a damper on things when needing to spend money. Joel was a total gentleman, though, and didn't even bat an eye when I told him the amount.

I smile as I think about that moment. It isn't often that I've felt like I was taken care of, like I wasn't made to question who I am or what my worth is. And in that moment, Joel did just that. A lifetime of friends bailing on me, parents not believing in me, and my ex-boyfriend making me feel less than at every opportunity he had...it all does a number on one's self-esteem.

So of course, I'm going to worry that Joel doesn't like the cabin I booked.

I try for one more glance, and this time, I linger. I study the crow's feet next to his eyes as they study the structure in front of us. The wrinkles remind me of our age difference, not that it's anything unheard of. But I wonder if right now he's thinking that he's made a mistake, that I'm too young for him. That I'm immature and have no class or style.

I clear my throat and gamble that my voice won't crack. I'm nervous, but I'm hoping he won't read into that.

"So?" I begin, then go for a complete sentence like a big girl. "What do you think?"

It's like he's snapped back into boyfriend mode, bringing the mask back up. I hate to think that way, but why not? A moment ago, he wasn't speaking, and now he's smiling. The wrinkles around his eyes are even deeper, and he looks at me with raised eyebrows.

"It's perfect," he says.

"I was worried that you thought it would be—"

"Not quite the cabin in the woods experience I was thinking?" he says, like he was reading my mind.

"Something like that," I say.

"It isn't," he says. "But that's perfectly fine. I'm just impressed that you found it for us. If the outside of the cabin ruins my trip, then there's something very wrong with me. Besides, I think we'll be lucky if we see the outside of this cabin again before the end of the trip, if you know what I mean." He followed that with a little wink, again reminding me of our age gap. Nobody in their twenties winks. At least, nobody I'd consider dating in that age range, of course.

"Good," I say. "And I do know what you mean." I give him a wink of my own, the muscles around my eyes rarely used that way. But if he's going to play the part of happy, understanding boyfriend, I can play my part, too.

"Should we take a look?" he asks, turning the key and pulling it out of the ignition.

I smile, and we step out of the vehicle, each of us having our own expectations of this trip, but neither of us knowing what we're truly in store for this weekend.

TWO

Pine needles crunch under my feet as soon as I take my first step forward. They're everywhere, littering the short concrete driveway that leads up to the cabin. It's cool outside, but nothing a light jacket doesn't fix. It's definitely not coat weather, nor is it Ugg boot weather, though I still find myself wearing a pair, anyway. I'm in it more for the style and comfort than the warmth, though my feet are sweating more than I'd like. The things we sacrifice for fashion.

The drive up here had been longer than either one of us had expected, mostly because of the many stops we'd decided to make on the way. Payson is an interesting enough town, and we had to drive through it to get up here. I was surprised to learn that Joel had never been there and wanted to explore some. That was fine with me. It had been a while since I'd gotten the chance to have fun with someone when there weren't any strings attached.

Another holdover from being with my ex, of course. And then there were all my friends, my family, and whoever else didn't stick around after. I thought they would have been different, but clearly, I just hadn't seen who they truly were until after things were over between us.

I frown for a moment as all the memories flood into my mind. It's not something I like to relive, but it's hard when everything reminds me of him, and of everyone I lost along with him. I'm not sure what happened to the idea of loyalty, but it's obviously not much of a thing these days.

At least, when it comes to me, that is.

"Everything okay?" Joel asks when we're halfway up the driveway, looking back toward me. He stopped to check on me, and that makes me smile again. It's a small gesture, but all my worries melt. For a short moment, anyway.

"Great, actually," I say. It's not really a lie, either. The detour of exploring what Payson had to offer was the perfect memory to make on the way up here. I may still be getting to know him, but from what I've been told and what I've seen for myself, it is clear that Joel is not like my ex. Even with all the bad I've been through, I know there is still plenty of time for me to experience good.

That's what my therapist tells me, and at this point, I believe her. If I didn't, then I wouldn't be here. Well, I'm sure I'd still be here one way or another. Just not as hopeful.

"Good. You coming?" Joel asks me, motioning with his head. "You have the code to get in, right?"

I nod and pick up the pace, meeting him and locking arms with him. As soon as I do, I can smell his musk mixed with the car's leather interior that has clung to his clothing from the long drive.

We left the luggage in the car, which is fine by me. When I go on a trip, I usually like to get a lay of the land, scope out the entrance before bringing in all my bags. This should be no different, and Joel seems to be thinking the same way.

We both reach the door, which is on the side of the house instead of facing straight out at the driveway. A few steps ahead, to the right of the door, is the fence for a backyard, if "backyard" is the appropriate word for a place like this. The land the cabin sits on is large, and there is no grass or lawn in sight. A raggedy wooden gate with a rusted latch at the top connects the fence to the house.

Joel looks at the front door and frowns. I follow his gaze and see he's staring at the lock and handle. "What's wrong?" I ask him.

"No keypad," he says. "You sure we're at the right place?"

I nod. "Nothing fancy like a keypad," I say. "Before coming up here, I had to stop by an office in the valley and get the key from them."

"Old school," Joel remarks, lifting his eyebrows. "Seems really inefficient, though."

I shrug. "Guess that's why it wasn't booked up and I got a good deal on it," I answer, sliding the key into the lock and turning it. It gives me a little bit of trouble, but after I apply a little more pressure, it clicks.

I'm not exactly sure what it is right now, but something feels off to me. I wonder if Joel can sense it, too. If he can, he doesn't let on. If I knew any better, I'd turn around and demand we leave right now.

But of course, that's not me. I'm already committed to being here, to spending this weekend here with Joel. Call it sunk cost fallacy or just not trusting my own gut, but either way, I twist the knob and push the door inside the cabin.

This might be the last normal thing that happens to us on this trip.

THREE

The door creaks and moans at the hinges, the seal from the outer edge breaks free, and a whoosh of air cuts in front of me before I can even take a step inside. A cloud of dust kicks up and stirs, finding its way into my nostrils before I have a chance to cover my nose. A sneeze builds up and escapes me, shooting a mist of air to combat the dust. Two more sneezes happen in rapid succession after. My eyes water, and I know this place won't be great for my allergies.

"Sheesh," Joel says from behind me. He scoots in around me, taking a step inside and giving me a look. I can tell he is unimpressed, and I have to admit, I don't blame him.

The inside is small but cozy. It's cute, that's for sure. A round table sits to the left of the door, a few chairs tucked underneath it. Next to that is a wood-burning stove, the chimney pipe stretching all the way up to the vaulted ceiling and, presumably, out the top of the roof. The small living area is beyond that, with a loveseat, chair, and television. A door is tucked to the side, leading to a bedroom downstairs.

Next to that door is the staircase, which runs right behind the television and leads up to the loft and master bedroom. To our right is the kitchen. It's fairly decent in size, considering the overall space. Past the fridge, there's a door leading to a bathroom.

It's not so much the size or the aesthetics of the cabin that puts either one of us off, but the cleanliness—or lack thereof. Not even counting the cloud of dust that stirred up upon our entry, I can spot a layer of it on every surface in sight. Beyond that, I can see a few corners where cobwebs have collected. I'm pretty sure there's a spider right underneath the wood-burning stove, a little black dot making its way around the legs of the stove, obviously not expecting anyone to be coming.

It's clear that the place hasn't been cleaned in a while. Not only has there not been anyone who's stayed here in some time, but nobody has been in to check on it, either. I had no idea it would be this bad.

"Where did you find this place again?" Joel asks me, scratching the back of his head.

Great, I think. Did I just ruin the entire plan by bringing him to this place? I guess I could have prepared better, but I figured it was the perfect spot. Out of the way, nobody to bother us, and in a cute little town.

"Sorry," I offer. "I didn't think it was gonna be this... well..."

"Rustic?" he says with a smile.

"Is that optimism?" I ask him. "'Cause I was pretty sure you were about to say we should go check in at the Best Western we saw on the way in."

Joel's chuckle sets my mind at ease. "Gotta be honest, it's not quite the experience I was expecting to walk in on."

I nod, lifting my eyebrows as I study the interior. "Me neither," I agree.

"But assuming it's just the untouched look and not somebody-pissed-the-bed-and-nobody-changed-the-sheets-look, then I don't think it's that big of a deal. Do you?"

I let out a long sigh. "I mean, I guess not."

"For sure message the company and complain, though. Maybe they can send someone to tidy up the place."

I nod slowly, thinking about how exactly that conversation will go, but I try to stay optimistic. "Why don't we do this—you go get the bags, and I'll start sweeping up, dusting the counters, and making sure that nobody pissed the sheets," I offer with a smile.

"You shouldn't have to clean up the place," he says, frowning. "It's on them to take care of it."

"Oh, don't worry, I'll take pictures of the before," I say. "They will definitely be giving us a discount. But with how old school they are, I have a feeling we'll be waiting a while for anyone to even come out here. And I don't know about you, but after that ride, I'm ready to get settled."

Joel groans, but finally nods. "Alright," he says. "I'll take a look in the backyard, too, make sure nothing is awry so we can make all the complaints at once. Hopefully, this is it, though."

"Let's hope," I say with a nod.

"I really didn't want you to have to clean on our weekend away, you know."

"I booked it, so it's the least I can do to salvage this trip."

He lets out a cackle. "If something small like dust and cobwebs is what ruins this trip, then what does that say about me? A hiccup is all it is."

He puts his arm around my waist and pulls me in, his lips locking against mine. He pulls back and smiles down at me before turning around and heading out through the door.

"I appreciate the optimism," I say. "Now, go check out the yard and then bring in the heavy stuff."

"Oh, now I see how it is," he teases from the doorway. "You wipe some surfaces, and I'm lugging all your bags up those stairs."

I smile and give a small shrug before closing the door in his face. I can hear his laughter through the solid wood, fading as he walks toward the backyard.

I turn around and survey the interior of the cabin again, letting out a long sigh. I know I'm the one who set this place up to stay in, but I didn't think I'd be cleaning it when we got here.

"Where do I even start?" I ask nobody. Maybe that spider under the wood stove has an answer, but if it does, it isn't sharing it. I laugh, thinking I should probably start cleaning by removing that little guy.

But before I can squat down to see where it might be hiding, a scream erupts from the backyard.

FOUR

After scrambling around inside and fumbling with the doorknob, I manage to get outside. I take a deep breath, feeling the fresh air fill my lungs once again, combating the stuffy air I was breathing only seconds ago. Blood rushes to my head, and I have to put a hand against the wall to steady myself so I don't fall down.

Panic.

It isn't the first time this has happened, but it has been a while. I thought I was doing so well, for a time, but the sudden burst of the unknown has shattered all the work I've done to this point. Questions run through my mind, each too fast for me to answer before it's gone and there's another one in its place.

Who is screaming? Is Joel in trouble? Is he hurt? Where is Joel? Do I need to be ready for a fight? Is someone coming for me? Why can't I figure out where the scream is coming from?

But I exhale, and somehow, things slow down enough that I can open my mouth. "Joel? Where are you?" I call out to the empty woods surrounding the cabin.

There's a deafening silence, except for a faint rumble. I can't place where it is, exactly, but it sounds very low, almost like an engine idling in the distance. Just before I can call out again, I hear Joel's voice cut in.

"Back here," he says. His voice is shaky, but he isn't shouting this time.

I rush to the gate for the backyard and find the latch. It's up high, but I can just reach it with my fingertips, lift it, and pull the gate open. The gate hits against the wall of the cabin, rattling as rebounds. I pay it no mind as I step onto the ground behind the cabin, searching for Joel.

It's pretty bare in the large area behind the building. A fire pit sits in the center of an open area of dirt, surrounded by a few navy Adirondack chairs. There is a tree in each corner of the property, but other than that, it's a wasteland. Certainly nothing special for anyone renting the place. But right now, I'm not too concerned about it.

"Joel?" I ask, not shouting this time.

"Back here," he says almost immediately, his voice coming from my left. The rumbling is louder now, and I hear feet crunching on gravel.

I spin on my heels, looking frantically for him, and spot just a small piece of his jacket. He is on the other side of the cabin, where the yard wraps around it. I pick my pace up to a jog, feeling a little relief now that I have eyes on him. Or at least, a smidge of him.

"What the hell are you doing?" I ask, approaching the corner of the cabin. "You scared the sh—"

Once I turn the corner, I immediately see the problem.

Joel has his hands raised outward, like he's trying to show he's unarmed and not a threat. Of course, the large black dog in front of him, baring his teeth and growling, saliva dripping from its mouth and onto the dirt, doesn't seem to care much.

That low rumble of what I thought was an engine continues, but much louder. The dog's upper lip quivers as he snarls. He lets out a single loud bark, and immediately, Joel lets out a yelp.

"Can you get a stick or something?" Joel asks.

"There's a pile of firewood in the opposite corner," I say, pointing right by the gate I walked in through. Just to the right of the gate is a large mound of wood, covered by a single blue tarp to prevent rain or snow from soaking it through.

"Anything big?" he asks.

I sour, realizing what he wants the wood for. "I'm not gonna hit the dog."

"Then what other suggestion do you have?"

My eyes dart around, and then I see where the animal came in through. Just behind the dog is a broken piece of fencing. Next to that is the pile of rocks and wood, plus a ladder lying flat that had been piled there to block it, which is clearly no longer doing its job. The rain, wind, and maybe even the dog pushing and digging against the barricade has done enough to expose the hole. Either that, or it wasn't a great blockade in the first place.

Whatever the case, the dog is here now. And Joel is scared to the point that he wants to get in a fight with the dog. That would be a very bad idea.

I shake my head, then take a deep breath. I step in front of Joel, putting myself between him and the dog, then clap my hands as firmly as I can. The sound is loud and cuts through the air like a sharp knife. It's just what I needed to break the dog's trance.

The dog stops growling and pulls his teeth back into its mouth. He looks at me, almost curious, tilting his head.

"Hey!" I yell at the dog, and it takes a single step backward, still curious. "Get out of here!" I command the dog with everything I have, pointing to the hole he clearly came in through.

I clap one more time, and something clicks inside the dog. He turns away and slips through the hole. I almost think he won't fit, but he manages to cram in, wriggle through, and disappear to the other side. I hear his footsteps pound further away until I hear them no more.

My heart is pounding in my chest when only moments ago, I couldn't have told you if it was beating at all. I watch Joel scurry to his knees by the fence and start to pile the wood and rocks into place to recreate the barricade that once was there. He props the ladder on its side, pressing it against the pile. He gives the fence a shake, checking to see if the pile will tumble over, but it doesn't. He seems satisfied enough with it as he climbs to his feet.

The look on his face, though, is something else. Concern? Disgust? Confusion? I'm not really sure.

"What was that?" he asked.

I shake my head. "What do you mean? Looks like the dog got in through the hole, which you just fixed."

He jerks his head toward the fence. "No, I mean the dog. How'd you do that? I was sure that dog wanted to rip me to shreds and wouldn't leave me alone no matter what I did. You just stepped into the line of fire and told him to leave."

I shrug. "I grew up with big dogs as a kid."

"Mean ones?"

"Asserting dominance is the key, I guess. Instincts just kicked in," I say. I don't really know how to explain it, but I feel like this makes the most sense.

He shakes his head in disbelief, maybe even relief. But a

part of me wonders if he feels like I've insulted his masculinity somehow.

"You okay?" I ask him.

He laughs with a nod. "I guess so," he says. "Thanks to you and your *dominance*." He has a sly smile across his lips. I suppose I haven't damaged his masculinity after all. In fact, maybe I've stirred something up.

"Good," I say. "Now I can go clean up—"

"Or we can put that on hold," he says, stepping close to me. "Maybe you can show me how you assert that dominance upstairs."

I feel the warmth of his body closing in on mine, and all I can do is take his hand to rush us upstairs, both of us quickly forgetting about the incident with the dog.

FIVE

The early stages of a relationship can be a mixed bag when it comes to sex. There's the nervousness, not being sure what the other person likes or wants. There's being self-conscious about revealing too much of what *you* like or want, and then just being unsure of yourself in general.

Will he notice the wonky little toe I have that juts out to the side? Will I be too sweaty? Will I move a way that he doesn't like? Is my stomach too squishy for him?

And so on...

Luckily, a few of those questions have been answered since this isn't our first time together. But it is our first time spending a weekend away together. And that means a lot more time to be around each other while we aren't in date mode.

Date mode is when he gets the few hours of me being fully put together, being "on" like I'm at a job interview. Even the sex is put on date mode during those times. It's like a performance in some ways. No, I don't mean faking it. It's almost hard to describe, but it's just that I can't unleash too much. I try to be as normal as possible, slowly letting more of my true self out each time.

But now for a whole weekend? That's not sustainable. And I'm not the only one who does this, either. I know it. Joel has to feel the same way. And he has his own rituals and procedures when it comes to his version of date mode.

But today? Oh my god. This is nowhere near "normal". Normal is good, normal is safe. But by playing it that way, it never gets great.

And holy crap, is it going great right now.

It's dark in the room, but I stare at the white ceiling where an outdated light fixture sits. One of those "boob lights", the round glass kind with a center point made of metal that looks like a nipple, sits up there completely turned off. It is the only thing turned off in this room, though, because right now, Joel is working wonders.

I look down and see the top of Joel's head between my legs. This is one of those moments when we've broken the date mode. I was just sitting in a car for hours, and now here he is, making good use of his tongue. I might normally feel self-conscious about it, but Joel doesn't seem to care at all. If he did, I don't think he'd be as enthusiastic as he is right now.

I roll my head back against the pillow, feeling a cool breeze from the air conditioner that sits just behind the low headboard behind my head. I manage to see a flutter of the blackout curtains that drape over the window and settle just on top of the air conditioner. Everything else in the room becomes a blur to me.

Unless it is in close proximity, I don't think I can see much of anything. It's been so long since I've felt this way. Not only has it been a while since I was with my ex, but near the end of the relationship, we rarely had sex that was this gratifying. For me, anyway. And after it all ended, I did everything I could not to let myself feel anything.

But now all I want to do is allow myself to feel *everything*.

I feel it building inside of me as Joel continues on, his tongue caressing gently against me, firmer at times and lighter at others. And when it clicks into the right pace, I feel his head start to pull away. Is he tired? Unsure?

I don't care, grabbing the back of his head and applying just enough pressure to encourage him, and then he catches on.

"Don't stop," I whisper greedily.

He follows my orders, and I keep pushing down on his head.

And then it happens.

I feel it build to the point of pushing me over the edge, and I just let go.

My legs shake, and I feel wave after wave wash over me. My skin is tingly, my heart is racing, and my blood is pumping through my body so fast that I'm burning hot. I lift my hips, his mouth following along, not letting up as I writhe around. My feet dig into the sheets, and my free hand flails around, gripping the back of the headrest as I ride the final wave.

And then it's over. I shift away from him, grabbing the top of his head and pushing it as I do. I'm far too sensitive to be touched right now, and I let out a long exhale. I open my eyes, not realizing I'd closed them at some point, and swallow.

"Where did that come from?" is all I can say.

"Turn over," he says. I was giving commands only moments ago, and now it's his turn. I don't argue; I don't say anything. All I can do is follow his instructions.

I feel his hands on my hips as I get on my knees, holding onto the headrest for stability, and then I feel him. This time, he is the greedy one, the forceful one, but in a good way. And I feel all of him as he thrusts against me.

The headrest is too low, and I nearly topple forward. He pulls back and starts his thrusts again. This time, my hands go higher, settling on top of the air conditioner, the cold air pushing against my sweaty palms.

He thrusts harder this time. It is borderline painful, but in a way I need, and I brace myself for it. My hands plant firmly on the air conditioner, and I stand my ground.

Until I don't.

I feel my brace give way, and not just a little bit. No, it's like the entire wall caves in, and I fling forward, my face hitting the upholstered headboard. My hands push all the way forward, finding their way into the cool air outside.

I hear Joel grunt, but I fall more forward than he expects, and he slips out of me. I hear something heavy smack against the wall and then a snap, followed only seconds later by a loud crash.

"What the hell was that?" Joel asks after a moment.

I pull my arms back, rubbing my chin where I hit the headboard. It's not painful, just more startling than anything. It's suddenly bright in the room from the window, and I see what's happened.

The air conditioner is gone. It had been sitting in the window only seconds ago. And now, well, it's not.

"Oh no," I say, stifling a laugh.

"No way," Joel says. I spin around to see him still on his knees, but staring at the open window, his jaw open in disbelief. "Did you just shove the air conditioner out of the window?"

I nod, still giggling. "I think so."

Joel closes his eyes, but he has a smile on his face. The absurdity of it all is comical, but we both know this trip is probably going to be more expensive than we planned.

"There goes the deposit," he says ruefully.

"Sorry," I say.

"Don't be," he says, lifting his eyebrows. "Causing property damage from sex was always on my bucket list."

I laugh and lean in to kiss him. Turning back to the window, I stick my head out to see how badly the air conditioner is busted. I don't have any delusions that it can be saved, but I'm curious.

But what I see isn't what I think either one of us would have expected from this situation. Because there's not just an air conditioner on the ground out there.

"Joel," I say, no longer laughing.

I feel his hands grabbing at my waist again, but I'm not in the mood. And once I tell him what I see, I know he won't be either.

"What is it?" he asks, concern in his voice.

"There's someone out there," I say. "I think the air conditioner landed on them. They're not moving."

SIX

The time between looking out the window and getting downstairs and outside in the backyard is a blur. I know the memories are there, but they are out of order.

There's us arguing. There's us rushing down the stairs. There's us putting clothes on. There's us both trying to look out the window. There's us fumbling with the lock and doorknob. There's us stopping in the dirt. There's us stepping on a power cord from the air conditioner. There's us scrambling off the bed.

Like I said, totally out of order. But the most important thing about it all is that it was *us* the whole time. United in this together. Which means that whatever it is we find in the backyard, we'll find it together.

Us figuring it out. Us facing it. Us leaning on each other.

That's the one thing that pushes me forward as I stare at the person in front of me.

I'm only feet away from the person—the woman—on the ground. She has blonde hair that covers half of her face. It looks like it would reach her shoulders if she were standing, but right now, it's all tangled in the dirt. And half of it is covered in deep red.

Her head is turned, facing our direction. I can make out a few features, like the purple eyeshadow she wears, her fair skin, her nose that is slightly longer than average. She's also older than me, maybe by ten years. I can't really tell, but she looks close to Joel's age.

I take a deep breath, once again realizing that I'm going to have to take control of this situation, just like with the dog earlier. Joel grabs my arm as I do, but not enough to actually stop me. I turn to him and nod before I take another step.

"I'm just gonna check," I say.

Joel only swallows as a response. Fear is in his eyes, which I understand. I just hope he doesn't shut down completely. Being a nurse, this situation is sort of in my wheelhouse. I deal with sick and injured patients every day. In my day to day, I just usually don't find them this...unresponsive. And definitely not outside of my workplace.

The ladder we had leaned against the fence is right by her, which tells me she moved it. The air conditioner lays right next to her, maybe six inches from her head, which doesn't take a forensic team to surmise is the reason she's on the ground. Of course, the reason she's here at all is still a mystery.

But that's not what I'm trying to figure out right now. No, right now, my job is to figure out how bad it is. Clearly, we should be calling 911, but I need to let Joel know how bad it is so he can relay that information.

I move the air conditioner with my foot. It's heavy, but now that half of its parts are scattered around the yard, it's a lot lighter than it used to be. I'm amazed that I was able to shove it out of the window in the first place. But maybe all it needed was the right amount of force.

I move the woman's hair out of the way so I can find her neck. "Be careful," Joel finally says, which might be insulting if I didn't already think he was in shock.

Ignoring him, I place my fingers against her neck, just to the side, where I should be feeling a pulse.

I wait. And then I wait longer.

I swallow hard, my breathing picking up the pace. I blink a few times and then pull my fingers off her neck. I stare at her for a moment, trying to see any movement.

And then, I look up at Joel.

"What?" he asks. "Is she okay?"

I don't say anything for what seems like an eternity, but then, somehow, I find my voice.

"She's dead," I say.

SEVEN

Joel doesn't say a word. He stares at me, blinking. I thought I had found my voice, but at this point, he's acting like I haven't said a word. Still waiting for me to announce the condition of the woman at my feet.

But at this point, even if he didn't hear me, he should have figured it out by now. Wouldn't I be scrambling to save her life if there were any possibility of doing so?

"Joel," I say, trying to snap him out of it. "Did you hear me?"

He still stares down at the woman beside me. He tilts his head, like he's fascinated by the dead woman in front of him. But he's not being morbid; it's clearly still all shock.

"Joel!" I shout this time.

And suddenly, he snaps his eyes up at me, shaking his head to alleviate whatever fog was in his head.

"She's dead."

"Are—are you certain?" he asks. "I mean, she can't be, right?"

This time, I do get offended. "I'm a nurse, Joel," I say. Something he should know if he had been paying attention to any of our conversations on our dates. "I think I can tell if someone is alive or not. And this woman is clearly dead."

I stand up, my knees aching from the squat I held while checking the woman's pulse.

Joel shakes his head, still in disbelief. I know it's difficult for people. Hell, even I can't stomach the idea, but now is not the time to fall apart. The last thing I need is to deal with a man who can't pull it together.

"It can't be," he says to himself. His voice drifts lower, but I catch another sentence. "Oh, god. It's Angela all over again." At least, that's what it sounds like to me, even though it was nearly all breath and no voice.

"Who's Angela?" I ask.

"Huh?" he snaps, like he didn't realize he was speaking out loud.

"You said this is like Angela all over again. What does that even mean?"

He shakes his head and waves his hand. "Nothing, nothing," he says. "I was just muttering nonsense or something. I—I'm just a little in shock, you know?"

I swallow and nod. I'll let this go, because right now, it's not important. Right now, what's important is dealing with the situation. And that means we need to call emergency services.

"You have your phone on you?" I ask him.

"Y-yeah, I think so," he says, fishing in his pocket and pulling out his phone.

"Call 911," I say. "We need to tell them there's been an accident and that—"

"What?" he asks, again in disbelief or shock, except he doesn't sound like he's in shock anymore. In fact, he sounds clearer than ever before.

"I said call 9 1 1. Get the police and an ambulance here. The longer we wait, the longer—"

"What? That she's going to stay dead?" he asks. "Think they can bring her back somehow? 'Cause correct me if I'm wrong, you being the nurse and all, but can they do that?"

"Do what?"

"Make someone who's dead not dead," he says, his tone clipped and impatient.

Now I'm the one who's in disbelief.

"No," I say. "But we still—"

"No, we don't," he says.

Disbelief be damned, I'm full-blown confused. "You don't want to call the police about this?" I point to the woman's corpse.

He shakes his head. "That's right. We can't call them," he says.

I am about to question everything right now, but he cuts me off before I can. "What are we gonna tell them?" he asks. "That we just killed a woman?"

"I'm pretty sure they'll be able to see that it's an accident," I say, motioning toward the body again.

"You and I may know that, but from an outsider's perspective, that's not what it's gonna look like, trust me. They will twist our story, our words, until it all fits their narrative."

"Joel, you sound absolutely crazy right now!" I say, exasperated.

"They'll think we murdered her," he insists.

"I'm pretty sure, in the history of murder, nobody's murder weapon of choice was an air conditioner! What, I just so happened to be at the window and was waiting for some random woman to come by, and then what? *Haha, joke is on you, lady!* And just shoved the air conditioner out?" The entire thing is ridiculous, and I feel stupid even putting it into words. "Do you know how *that* sounds?"

After a moment, Joel nods. "Yeah, it sounds stupid."

"Then call them," I say.

But he shakes his head. "I can't, Stella," he says.

"Fine," I say, now fully pissed at him. I jerk my phone out of my pocket, waving it in his direction. "Then I will."

Maybe my irritation has me off-guard, but I never thought I ever had reason to be on guard with Joel. When someone gets hurt, I always thought the entire world would agree that you're supposed to call for help. Unless you're a maniac or serial killer, of course.

And while I don't think Joel is either of those things, I'm beginning to question *who* exactly he is. Because just before I can pull my phone to punch in the three numbers, he snatches it right out of my hand.

My eyes go wide, and I'm at a loss for words. I was holding it together pretty well before, but the shock hits me full force.

So much for *us* in this together. Right now, I'm feeling very *alone* in this thing.

He's standing there, checking that I didn't dial 911, but I hadn't gotten the chance to call the authorities. And now I'm wishing I had, not only to tell them about this woman, but also to get out here because of the way Joel is acting right now. He is not acting like the man I drove up here with for a romantic getaway.

He's sweating, mumbling to himself while double-checking my phone. His eyes dart around the yard and back to the woman on the ground.

And what *was* that comment about Angela, anyway?

Finally, I find my voice, knowing I'm not one to usually let a man treat me like this. It's a high-stress situation, so I'm willing to give him a pass, but he's going to have to clear some things up. And he's going to have to do it right now.

"What the hell are you doing?" I demand. "You know how bad this is gonna look if we don't call the police? You're not acting right in the head."

Joel swallows and locks his eyes on me. He takes a deep breath, and I can see the wheels spinning in his head. Like he's not sure if he should say something, or even worse, like he's trying to craft a lie. I've seen that look before with my ex countless times.

But finally, he relents. He must have figured out he couldn't spin this situation in his favor. Which is good, because I'll see right through any lie he tries to come up with.

But the next thing out of his mouth isn't anything I would have expected in this or any other situation.

"We can't call the police," Joel says, "because that's Emily. My wife."

EIGHT

Emily
Earlier today

Dealing with insurance is the worst part of my job. I try to only do it once a week, filing the required paperwork for each person. Most of the time, there isn't an issue. But every so often, there is a snag. One company tries to push back, and another might say they won't cover an appointment. It's tiring, and was hardly talked about the entire time I was in school.

But I suppose it's worth doing to reap the benefits of my job. I love helping people, and in return, I feel like it helps me. It's therapeutic, even.

My desk is a stack of papers, neat and tidy on the right side, but the left is a little more haphazard. Those papers are stacked, but just in a pile I can work through quickly, which, when done, gets placed on the right side. At the end of the day, the desk will look perfect and in order.

Another thing I enjoy doing—the organization of it all. Around my office, everything is arranged just the way I like it. The small chair tucked in the corner with the peace lily on the table next to it, sitting just under the pendant floor lamp. The paintings I hand-picked from the farmers' market by a local artist, whose work is severely underpriced. And the small sound machine for the low-level white noise that helps me focus and stay grounded.

My office is a bit of a sanctuary. Not much of anything can break that.

There is always, of course, the lingering nag. My computer screen is open, and I see that one email that always eats at me. I open it and take a look, reading through the words of a woman I never met. And one I never will. Her heartbreak, her sadness, her accusations. It's why I do this job, but I can't always help everyone.

My phone chimes on my desk, preventing me from going down that rabbit hole too far—again. Usually, I hate distractions, but this time, it's a much-needed one.

I usually have my phone on do not disturb, so this call must be from an app I don't normally check. One of the old apps that somehow slipped through the cracks.

I swipe at my phone, thinking about dismissing it immediately, but my curiosity is piqued when I see it's an alert for gaining points at the grocery store. Points I've accumulated because of recent purchases.

But I didn't make these purchases. It must have been Joel. My husband told me about his business trip this weekend, so he must be buying items for the upcoming road trip he has to take. That's fine, of course. It's not like I'm monitoring the account or anything.

I click the app to see the points in depth, but freeze when I notice a breakdown of what he purchased.

And that's when I see this business trip might not be quite as *business* as Joel led me to believe.

Two items on the receipt stand out to me. Champagne, which might not be so unusual. It's very possible Joel wants to pop open a bottle tonight and share it with me, maybe make a whole romantic night out of it. Of course, that would be out of the ordinary for him because the last romantic night he planned for us was our anniversary, and he had a two-for-one coupon at a chain steakhouse a mile away from the house.

But it's the second item I can't explain away. Condoms. Why the hell would he need those? Because his explanation of using them with me would only be negative.

I quickly pull up my bank account, trying to see the charges for the grocery store. Just as I thought, there aren't any. Nothing on the account, and nothing on the credit card. The only evidence is the app.

Joel went through all the trouble to pay cash for these things so that he could go out for the weekend with some little tartlet and not get caught. But when presented with the opportunity to earn reward points, the cheap bastard couldn't help himself.

The idiot didn't think about the phone number being tied to it and that I would get an alert with everything that he bought.

I clench my fists on top of my desk, anger building up inside me. So much for my office sanctuary. Few things can break it, but I'd say a cheating husband might be at the top of the list.

Now *his* business trip lie has become *my* business.

"You piece of—" I grit my teeth, not allowing myself to go off the rails. Being angry about the whole thing isn't going to do me any good. And to be honest, this is no surprise to me. I'm more pissed about his stupidity than anything else.

I know his smug little face is thinking he's getting away with all of it. Having his cake and eating it, too.

But he's clearly not as smart as he thinks he is.

And then a smile creeps across my face. Because I'm not going to get angry. What good will that do? I could confront him about it when he gets home, and he could come up with some half-baked lie and try to gaslight me by making me believe I'm paranoid and making false accusations.

So no, I won't do that.

I'm going to have to do more. A way that he can't deny my accusations.

Like catching him in the act.

Can't really argue with someone seeing it with their own eyes, can you? And then what will he come up with? I have no idea, but I'm sure he'll try.

And I can't wait to see him fail miserably at it.

NINE

The biggest hurdle I run into is finding where they started from. At least, that's what I think the biggest issue will be. Really, it was much easier than I thought when I got to the grocery store. There are a few locations of this grocery store spread out through the valley, but the one Joel stopped at told me all I needed to know about the direction they were headed.

It is on the outskirts of town, and unless they were planning on heading to Apache Junction—though, whoever is?—then they'd be heading up Usery Pass and the 87 highway that leads right to Payson. After that, it could go anywhere if they were planning to keep on, but I figure I've got the whole road to find Joel and whoever he's truly with.

But much to my surprise, I don't even have to try that hard. I figured I'd have to dart around from car to car, trying to find Joel's vehicle. Maybe even rely on some sort of way to track his phone, though I'm sure Joel has already covered that one. Instead, all I have to do is look to the far left at the corner across the street from the grocery store plaza, which is where I spot Joel's gunmetal-gray hatchback.

Just seeing the color of the thing reminds me how excited he was to find it. Like the shade was a key selling point for him. I'm all for liking color, but Joel associated it with much more than just something he liked. It was almost like he thought of it as connected to being a man.

Many times in our marriage, Joel was not the most emotionally mature person. But I put up with it because I thought that was what I was supposed to do. My lot in life was to change him.

And other than me becoming aware of that fact, I don't know if anything has changed.

Staring at the vehicle across the street, I can see Joel putting away the nozzle for the gas and getting back inside the vehicle. Next to him is a woman. I can't make out any of her features other than that she is clearly sitting next to him. And then I see Joel lean over and give her what I assume is a kiss.

I don't know if I'm even angry anymore because I'm so thrilled to catch him in the act. Maybe I could go up to them now, ask him what the hell he thinks he is doing with her in the car. But I think he would still try to explain it away.

I work with her. I'm just giving her a ride. That wasn't a kiss you just saw. You're being paranoid. Do you really not trust me enough that you'd follow me all this way?

All those questions and answers could pop up on his end, and I wouldn't have much of a rebuttal. Or at least one I think would convince him that I've caught him. And that's the goal, right? Not just to know I've caught him, but to put him in a position where I've cornered him so much, he *has* to break.

So, no. I'll wait and see.

I watch as Joel starts up his car, then pulls out of the lot and onto the road. He's headed up north, which is exactly what I thought he would do. That man is so predictable sometimes. Even if I hoped he wasn't.

After checking for traffic, I pull onto the road, keeping my distance a few cars behind him. I don't need to follow so closely now that he's confirmed my suspicions of where they're headed, but I also don't want to lose them. Once they get to Payson, all bets are off on what they'll do, so I need to be ready and stay close.

And then I can give Joel the surprise of his life.

TEN

The ride to Payson is actually kind of nice. Normally, on a ride like this, I'd be irritated that traffic was slow. Some of the roads leading to the main highway are single, winding lanes that people act like are the most dangerous routes in the world, driving twenty miles under the speed limit.

Those people are still frustrating as hell, but since it's not *my* trip to Payson that's getting delayed, I'm in no rush. I can see Joel's vehicle a few cars up, stuck behind one of the many slow drivers, and we're all going to get where we're going at whatever pace is happening. Plus, this way, I get to finish my audiobook.

Who knew that Joel's little cheating escapade would grant me the free time I needed to pursue some of my hobbies? I smile, knowing I could smugly thank him for this opportunity. I can't wait to lay it on thick.

Being a bitch when someone deserves it is one of my favorite things. And I'd say Joel deserves it more than ever right now.

But I'll have to wait, take my time with it. Can't rush

into anything now, can I? Just like these drivers on the road. We'll all get there eventually.

And Joel will definitely know when I do.

Eventually, the highway opens up and we're moving at a quicker pace, but Joel doesn't seem interested in speeding too much. He's driving only a few miles above the speed limit, staying in the right lane, not trying to pass anyone.

Maybe he's trying to avoid a ticket so he wouldn't have to craft another lie, but I don't think he's smart enough to think ahead that much. Either he just doesn't want to pay a fine, or he's having too good of a time talking to that little tartlet next to him.

That's fine, too, because I don't need to stress. I'm able to keep a few cars between us, and once we all arrive at Payson, I can follow them around town.

It's busy for the weekend, I can already tell. And unfortunately for me, it looks like Joel is in no rush to get to whatever hotel he's reserved. No, he probably wants to impress this girl by buying her something nice. Something seemingly expensive, but nothing he can't swing. Partly because he has a nice job, but also because we share finances and *I* have a nice job.

Of course, he's already pulled all the cash out of our joint account. I already saw the few thousand he had withdrawn for "travel", or at least, that is what I'm sure he would tell me if I asked. But we both know this is not the kind of work-related travel he would want me to believe.

He just doesn't know that I know, too.

So, I take a little jaunt along with them. I pull off the same highway they do, pull onto the same smaller streets, and even into the same parking lot. Of course, I keep myself at a safe distance the whole time to make sure that Joel never spots me. I'm no secret agent or ninja, able to lurk around and not make my presence known. In fact, I'm probably terrible at this. But Joel is so wrapped up in this girl, and seemingly so impressed with his own lie, he can't even fathom that I would be on to him.

I'm almost sorry for him. And a little irritated at myself for ever finding something worthwhile in him in the first place.

But I don't let those feelings keep me down. Instead, I watch the pair as they enter a little boutique. I can see the girl a little more clearly now, enough to notice she has blond hair and a thin figure. I don't go into the same shop because *I'm* smart enough to know I don't have the skills that might take to go unnoticed. And sure, if I were noticed, I'd catch Joel red-handed. Though his denial would be pretty weak, I want to catch him *my way*.

I walk into a candle shop, not really focusing on anything specific. Just rummaging around here and there, always keeping an eye on the pair—or is it *couple* at this point? I don't know for sure, but whatever the case, when I see them through the window, they must be one because the lengths Joel is going to make it happen is way more than I've ever experienced myself. Hands on her waist, lips on lips, even their hips grinding in places. They shouldn't be in a public place at all.

Joel is a damn horn dog. For other women, of course. I suppose I'm not new or exciting enough these days. I guess I've always known this in some ways about him; I've just never seen it with my own eyes like this before.

The day goes on like this. They pop into a different store along the street, and I follow them, in the store they previously visited. I keep my distance, watching, until they get to the end of the street where the shops end. And then they double back toward the car.

I stay hidden behind some racks in the handmade soap shop, but can't help but steal a much closer look at the two of them together. They're both smiling, like they're enjoying the day. The girl is cute but young, which just makes me roll my eyes. Joel can't even be original with how he cheats. Just another scumbag middle-aged man who wants young and new.

It's kind of gross when I think about it.

I let them pass and slowly follow behind. I hang out at the corner, letting them get into their car and drive to the main road before scurrying across the parking lot and into my own car. I only have a small window, but I manage not to let them get ahead too far.

As we drive, my idea of a hotel room in Payson is put to rest when we get on the 260 highway and head through Forest Lakes. We cross a terribly paved street that I can't believe doesn't cause many accidents and then proceed to Heber-Overgaard.

I've never been here before, and to be honest, it doesn't look like much from my vantage point on the highway. But there are some cute places on the side of the road, like a lavender shop, a small market, a few eateries, and some strange mural about aliens and phone booths. I'll have to look that one up when I get home.

Eventually, through a series of turns and twists on some paved roads and some unpaved roads, we reach a small neighborhood of cabins. They're spaced out far enough to offer a lot of privacy to whoever stays in them.

I start to give them a greater distance at this point because it'll be far more obvious that someone is behind them without the heavier traffic. And despite how dumb Joel is, I think even he could make out that the car behind him is his wife's. So, I don't let him see me and keep a full street behind. The cloud of dust in the air on the dirt road leaves enough of a trail that I can find them without actually following them.

One last pathway, not even really a road at this point, and I can see them in the distance. Joel's car is pulled up in a driveway, and they're standing outside a small but modern-looking cabin. It's cute, and I bet it would make a great little spot for a weekend getaway.

I'm sure Joel thinks so, too.

But he doesn't know what's coming for him, does he?

I smile as I find a spot to pull over that doesn't seem conspicuous and watch them from afar. They go inside the cabin, then back outside. I don't really hear much, but they spend some time in the back of the cabin for a brief moment. I'm alone with my thoughts, so I could be anywhere with them, but all I can do is think about Joel's stupid face when it's all over.

When they reemerge from the back of the cabin, Joel can barely keep his hands off the girl. I feel a little sorry for her. She could do much better than him, and I'm sure she knows it. Hell, maybe Joel does, too, hence his eagerness to get her back in the cabin.

I wait a few minutes before stepping out of my car. The look on his face tells me everything I need to know about his intentions. I doubt they're coming back out right away. At least, not unless Joel reaches the end sooner than he intends.

That thought alone makes me laugh.

I make my way across the street and past his vehicle. I take a look in the back and see their stuff through the window. They couldn't even unpack before getting down to business. Ah, the thrill of a new relationship. All so fresh and raw.

I can't wait to tear it all down.

The door is just up ahead. It's painted teal, or maybe more of a turquoise color? I can't really tell the difference, not that it matters. But I stand in front of it, thinking about knocking, then stop myself.

That wouldn't be enough, would it, to knock and give them a chance to cover themselves up? Or hell, even ignore me. I need something concrete. Not just for me, but for Joel. I'd love to see him try to talk his way out of being balls-deep in some tartlet.

No, I can't just knock and have him answer. That's not the plan, and to be honest, it never really was.

I have to *literally* catch them in the act.

I step back from the door and turn to the gate leading to the backyard. I unlatch it and step into the large area behind it. If I were in a different mindset, I'd turn my nose at the digs back here. A rickety fire pit and some plastic chairs don't scream "romantic getaway" to me, but leave it to Joel to muck that one up.

Still, not my problem.

In the cabin, I hear Joel making quick work upstairs as his little tartlet becomes audible through the window upstairs. Whatever he's doing seems to be doing wonders for her, and as much as I try not to, I can imagine exactly what he's up to. I don't hear any vocalizations from him, which means his tongue is probably busy elsewhere.

I clench my teeth as the image enters my mind, and anger swells inside me again. I need to hurry and figure out how to get up there to give him the surprise of his life.

Peering up to the second floor, I use my hand as a visor to block the little bit of sun in the sky. There is some cloud coverage, but it still peeks through enough to be irritating. The window seems small from here, but I can see the air conditioner in the lower half, telling me it's just the distance that dwarfs it. It's too high, and the wall is completely flat, so I can't scale it. I need to find something that can get me up there.

I spot it as soon as I lower my eyes from the window. It's like it was meant to be. Around the corner of the cabin is a ladder. I can just make out the feet of the metal structure. It's on its side, leaning against the fence.

I pull at it, dragging it a little toward me, then grab it in the center and prop it up to my side. It's not as heavy as I thought it would be, but it's long enough that it looks like it will reach the window. And that's all I need it to do.

I stand just under the window, maneuvering the ladder around before I take one more look up at the window. I narrow my eyes, noticing the air conditioner wobble slightly. I swallow, knowing that it's now or never.

I pull the ladder just along the wall, and then that's when I see it.

The air conditioner falling from the window, headed straight down, to right where I'm standing.

ELEVEN

Joel
One month ago

Parking is just as irritating as it always is whenever I swing by the medical center. It's like whoever constructed this place decided to cram as many offices inside it as they could so every type of private-practicing doctor could work out of it. They didn't think about just how many employees and patients would be present at the same time.

The list of doctors on the directory is so big that it needs two sides. There are doctors for your stomach, doctors for your feet, doctors for your head—in fact, different types of head doctors. Ones who deal with skulls, others that deal with brains, and the ones who deal with your mental health. The list goes on and on, and I don't even know all the specific names for certain specialties.

Thank god nobody is testing me on this directory because I'd fail miserably. Instead, I'm here for only one person. And as much as I keep telling her to move her office, she never does.

Oh, well, I think to myself. I found a parking spot, so now I just have to walk the outdoor maze of office doors until I find where I'm supposed to be. I've done this walk numerous times now, but still always somehow manage to get lost along the way. That's why I always glance at the directory as a refresher before heading into the plaza.

Once past the directory, I'm in the open courtyard and the sun is shining straight down on me. It's almost pleasant here, reminding me of a park with tables and ramadas for people to sit around, eat lunch, maybe take a break and read. Of course, I'm reminded about the space that could have been used for parking, but that's a moot point. A pathway leads straight through it, and along the edges of the courtyard, various office doors surround it. I head in that direction.

"Oh, you've got to be kidding me!" I hear a woman growl from the corner of the courtyard.

She's the only person outside, sitting at a picnic table just outside of where the sun hits.

She has blond hair that falls in front of her face while she stares at an iPad. She quickly runs a hand through it, tucking it behind her ear. It refuses to stay there and drifts back into its former place, where she quickly repeats the process. This time, it takes.

She wears a thin cream sweater, even though the weather seems a touch on the warm side for it. I find myself staring at her and admiring her natural beauty. She's maybe a decade younger than I am, which is evident by the lack of wrinkles around her eyes and the tight skin of her cheeks and down her neck. The kind of tightness untouched by a surgeon. And it's in the girlish way she sits, with her feet propped up on the bench instead of flat on the ground.

She glances up quickly from her tablet and suddenly locks eyes with me. I offer a quick, closed-mouth smile like I'm passing a coworker I'm not interested in speaking to. But to be honest, that couldn't be farther from the truth. I just don't want to come off as a creep. I've already been caught staring at her.

But she doesn't seem to mind. Instead, her eyes go back to the tablet, and I keep on toward the end of the courtyard. She lets out a long sigh, which is practically an invitation for me to speak up. To insert myself into her life. Her world.

I clear my throat subtly, just enough to draw her attention. "Tech problems are the worst," I say, second-guessing myself for a second.

But she doesn't cringe or pull back. Instead, she takes the invitation to open up.

"Are you good at that kind of thing?" she asks, her expression hopeful.

I stop walking and turn to her, this time not averting my eyes. "Depends on the issue," I say. "But yeah, probably."

Her eyes go wide, and she smiles, clearly relieved. "Thank god. I was about to tear my hair out if I had to try one more time."

A corner of my mouth lifts in a smile, and I make my way toward her. "I mean, you might be able to pull off the bald look, but I think you look great as you are now," I say.

It's a line, and I know it. Hell, she knows it. But her cheeks go pink, and she smiles again.

"So what's the issue?" I ask.

"This one app keeps sending me constant updates. I try to turn it off, but no matter what I do, they keep coming."

I immediately see the problem as she walks me through

it. The poor girl is in the wrong section altogether. Tech isn't my job, but I understand enough of it, given my daily use. "May I?" I ask, motioning toward the iPad.

She shoves it into my hands. "Please do."

I decide to walk her through the solution in case this happens again and I'm not around. "It's here in the general settings. Go here, then you can fix the notification settings," I say.

"That's it? I can't believe I couldn't figure that out," she says, being harder on herself than necessary. "I feel like a boomer or something with how technologically challenged I can be sometimes."

"I'm sure you're great at other things I can't even fathom," I say, trying to make her feel better. "But as an elder millennial, I'm happy to help."

She laughs. "Elder? You don't seem that old." Her laugh is light but genuine. Her voice alone makes me feel younger. I feel an excitement I haven't felt in a while.

This is an unexpected turn, but clearly, outside of some flirtation, this is where it ends. She's going to get back to her tablet, and I'm going to head to the offices. "Now that this is all figured out, I can get an Uber," she says.

I can't help myself, wanting to continue the conversation just a little longer with the beautiful woman. "Where you headed?"

"Just going to get some lunch, finally."

I nod, knowing that's my cue to let her be. "Fair enough. Enjoy!" I say, keeping my tone as upbeat as I can, though I'm a little disappointed to leave her.

"Hey," she says, stopping me from leaving. "This might be kind of weird, but you wanna get a burrito with me? There's this place a few blocks down that's awesome. I could use the company." The way she says that last line cures me of thinking that her flirtation was meaningless.

I hesitate, looking toward the gauntlet of offices. "I... uh..."

"Sorry! I went too far, didn't I? Forget I said anything," she says quickly, turning away and dropping her hair back into her face.

"No," I say, scrambling to keep the invitation open. "I'd love to join you. Let me just send a quick text."

She flashes me another smile, no longer embarrassed. I return the smile as I pull my phone from my pocket and find Emily.

Sorry, babe, something came up, I type. *Not gonna be able to make it to lunch today. Love you!*

I hit send, looking at the image of my wife on the screen. I hesitate only for a moment, wondering if this is the right thing to do. I know the answer to that, but when am I ever truthful with myself?

Before I can dwell on it, the young lady next to me chimes in. "Everything good?" she asks.

I shove my phone in my pocket. "Perfect," I say. "I'm Joel, by the way."

"Stella," she says, standing up from the bench. I was already close to her, but when she stands up, we are much closer now, and I can feel the spark of energy between us. "You ready?" she asks.

"Let's do it," I say, knowing my answer isn't just about grabbing lunch.

TWELVE

Joel
Present day

"Joel!" Stella yells. "Joel!"

I hear her yelling at me, but it sounds so much farther in the distance, even though she's standing only a few feet in front of me. My wife's body is on the ground, her head bloody, and she's not moving. The next thing that runs through my mind is exactly what just happened, but it feels so unreal.

Stella, the woman I have been seeing behind Emily's back, just told me that my wife is dead.

There are so many questions I can't answer. What is Emily even doing here? How did she get here? And then some more random ones, like what are the odds that she would even be in this spot right when an accidental push of the air conditioner happened?

It would just be my luck that this happened, wouldn't it?

Stella snaps her fingers in my face, and suddenly, her voice is louder and she's right in front of me. "Joel!" she screams, and I focus on her, present and aware.

"Stella," I say. This seems to do the trick, convincing Stella that I'm part of the conversation again.

"What do you mean, *your wife*?!" she demands.

It's right now that I realize how loud she is being. We aren't super close to the other properties, but we aren't all that far away, either. And in a place like this, with all the silence of the outdoors and without any traffic on the nearby road, I'm more than positive that noises carry.

I hold a hand up. "Shhh," I say to her, needing to gain control of this situation. There are a lot of moving parts right now, and I'm not even sure where to begin.

But I've already messed up because that wasn't quite the response Stella was looking for.

"Don't you dare shush me," she hisses, though she keeps her voice down. I think she finally realized just how loud she was being as well. Neither of us needs the attention before figuring out what our next move is.

"I'm sorry," I say, keeping my hand up. "Okay? I'm sorry. I didn't mean to shush you."

"*That's* what you're sorry for?" she hisses again.

I take a deep breath and let it out in a long sigh. This is going to be an ordeal, isn't it? No matter what I say, it's going to be picked apart. I know this, but I also know we have a much bigger situation at hand than anything Stella can accuse me of right now.

"No," I say. But already, she's opening her mouth again, so I can't let her have the chance. "Okay, yes, but also about not telling you that I—"

"Have a wife?" she finishes for me.

I nod. "Yeah. That I have a wife," I say. And I can't help but wonder if I should have said "had a wife" instead.

Semantics that I don't have time for at this point.

"Oh, I bet you are," Stella says, crossing her arms. "Now, give me my phone back."

I realize I'm still holding her phone in my other hand. I look down and think about it. I don't want to be *that* guy, but I also can't let her call the police. "Look, I'll give you your phone back, but we can't call the police, okay?" I say gently.

"Sure," she says tersely. "Whatever you say."

That is not the tone of someone who sounds like they're going to follow directions. In fact, it sounds like a passive-aggressive agreement so that they can immediately do the opposite of what I'm asking of them.

"Stella, if you call the police, this won't just be bad for me," I warn.

"Really?" she asks, narrowing her eyes at me. "Because I don't know this woman." She motions at my wife's lifeless body. "And if the police come here, they'll see it's an accident. Maybe you have things to explain, but—"

"They'll see the two of us together," I point out.

But that's not enough for her. She just shakes her head, not getting it.

"And I'm cheating on my wife with you," I add. It's the first time I've said it out loud, and in some ways, it feels like a ton of bricks hitting me. I feel like I'm the bad guy here, but I'm not the bad guy. I've just not been the greatest guy, right? But I have to lean into it right now. "And now my wife is dead." Another ton of bricks collapses on me as I say it out loud.

"It's clearly an accident," Stella repeats. She's so

focused on the truth that she can't see what the police will see.

"Is it, though?" I say.

She twists her face, like she's asking what the hell I mean.

"Or were you pissed off that you had to share me with her?" I continue. "How did she know we were here in the first place? And you *were* the one to shove the air conditioner out the window. Maybe you just wanted her out of the way." I lay it on thick, and even as I say the words, they sound a little far-fetched. But it's enough.

"What are you even talking about?" she asks, throwing her hands up. "I didn't even—"

"I know," I cut her off. "But you have to make *the police* believe that. They'll be looking at every angle, and once they find one, they won't let it go. Like a dog with a bone, I swear it. Haven't you watched any true crime documentaries?"

Emily loved to watch those shows, and I've seen a few myself because of her having them on all the time. I don't know for sure, but I'd be willing to bet that Stella watches them, too. There's something about women and true crime. I just don't get it.

And right as rain, Stella nods slowly. I knew it.

"But that doesn't—" she begins.

I don't even know what she's going to say next, but the fact that she's teetering is enough that I need to keep pushing. If the police come here, it will be bad for me. And I'm not *really* lying about how bad it will be for Stella, either. Accident or not, there is a lot of truth to what I'm telling her.

"On top of that, the rental is in your name alone, right?" I say. "Not mine. So, if anything, you call the police, and this is all on you." A little part of me feels bad about that one, but it's necessary.

"What are you saying?" she asks. "Are you threatening me—"

"No," I interject, approaching Stella and putting my hands on her arms. I don't pull her into a hug because I don't know how that will be met, but she seems to tolerate me touching her, which means I'm getting somewhere. "Not at all. I'm just laying out how it all might look when they dig in. Because I'll have to tell them the truth, too, and that includes you renting this place. You picked it."

Though Stella is young, I don't want to make the mistake of thinking she's dumb. But she sure is impressionable, and I'm going to use that to our advantage right now. And if I have to imply that I might steer the police to look at her for murder, then so be it. I won't come right out and say that, not unless she makes me. But not calling the police will also benefit her, even though I feel like a total scumbag doing it.

Because right now, covering my ass is far more important.

And cheating on my wife is only scratching the surface as far as what I've been keeping from Stella.

THIRTEEN

"We need to cover the body up right now," I say to Stella.

She's already agreed that we won't call the police, but I can tell that she's not happy with me. *Fair enough,* I think. But now, time is of the essence. Getting over the hurdle of not calling the authorities was the easy part. Now that we've agreed not to do that—well, more like now that I've pressured her not to do that—the last thing we want is to get caught with the body.

Because there's no explaining that one away, and if that happens, we would have been better off taking our chances calling the police in the first place.

But I'm confident that we won't find ourselves in that pickle. I haven't seen a soul since coming up to the cabin, and I haven't heard any cars around. As far as I can tell, we're completely alone. Sure, there are other homes within visible range of here, but that doesn't mean anything. There is plenty of tree coverage on the sides of the yard, and the home right behind our cabin is silent. I wouldn't be surprised if it was another vacation rental and nobody had rented it for the weekend.

Really, this is the perfect spot to take care of something like this. Of course, this would be my first time attempting to bury a dead body, but if I start second-guessing myself now, then I know we'll start having problems. Especially if Stella catches wind that I'm flying by the seat of my pants on this thing.

Fake it till you make it, I guess.

On top of that, Stella seems to be pretty good at this so far. She's the one who held it together when we found Emily's body, though I feel like my initial reaction was warranted, considering I wasn't expecting to see my wife here, let alone dead because of some freak accident. And even after finding out I was married, Stella seems to be taking the news as well as she can in a situation like this.

Once more, she's showing me that she handles pressure a lot better than I would have anticipated. In fact, she's already figured out how to hide the body for the time being.

Stella removes the few pieces of wood holding down the tarp above a huge stack of firewood. Once they're off, she pulls the tarp like a magician yanking a tablecloth from a table. A single piece of wood rolls off the stack and lands on the dirt with a thud. She trots back to Emily's body, holding out the tarp, a small breeze catching it and lifting the bottom, making a crinkling sound.

"Hopefully, it doesn't rain," I say, checking out the now fully exposed firewood. I know it's stupid the moment I think it, but it comes out of my mouth, anyway. Sometimes, I just can't help myself. It's something Emily had always pointed out, how critical I can be, and especially in moments like these where I wasn't being helpful at all. It's not like I was offering a better solution.

Stella seems to agree about that, too, because the look she gives me is anything but patient. "I think some wet firewood is going to be the least of our worries," she says. "But you're also right. Hopefully, it doesn't rain, but if it does, the tarp serves two purposes." She holds the blue plastic out to me. I take it, feeling a hint of shame.

"Thanks," I say, but my voice is muffled. I'm not even sure Stella even heard me because she's already walking around the other side of Emily's body.

"Let's lay the tarp down here next to her," Stella says, already squatting down and putting her corner of the tarp on the ground.

"Why not just cover her first?" I ask.

Stella sighs. "Like you pointed out, I hope it doesn't rain," she says. "But if it does, she'll be laying right in the mud." Stella looks up, and I follow her gaze. Dark clouds fill the sky in the distance, and it's clear they are headed our way.

I had to open my mouth, didn't I?

"Okay," I say, placing down my corner of the tarp on the dirt. Stella straightens out the tarp so it's flat. I watch as she focuses on the task at hand, still keeping it all together. How she's able to be so level-headed about the whole thing, especially after being convinced not to call the police, is a mystery to me. Right now, I don't know if I could be doing any of this without her.

"Now, we'll just roll her over the tarp once, and then we can wrap it around her the other way," Stella says.

And this is where I have a problem. I stare at her, then glance to Emily's body. I'm the one who came up with the idea to bury the body, but now I can't even bring myself to touch Emily. It's like the whole thing has just become real, and now I'm second-guessing everything.

But I can't cave now. Maybe we could convince everyone it

truly was an accident, even if they discover I've been cheating on my wife, but I'm sure that luck wouldn't hold. The police would still have to run my background, and departments talk. And if they do, they'll have a whole lot more questions for me after they see what happened with Angela, and how I'm linked to her. Even though that wasn't my fault, either.

I close my eyes, trying to shove those memories out of my head. I don't need to relive that nightmare right now. I haven't thought about her in a while, and then this happens, and now I'm saying her name to a woman I've only known for a month.

So much for all the work I've done to get over it.

"Joel," Stella says, snapping me out of my own thoughts once again.

"I—I'm sorry, Stella," I stutter. "I can't do this part." I hold my hands up and shake my head, trying to look as apologetic as I can.

Stella glares at me, and to be honest, I don't blame her. "You're kidding me," she says, though her tone is far from amused. "You're the one who wanted to do this."

"I know, but this part, I—I just can't," I stammer. "Cheating or not, this is still my wife. I still have feelings for her. It's not like I'm some cold-blooded killer who wanted this to happen." I'm know I'm pleading with Stella. And I know that telling the woman I was inside of only moments ago that I still have feelings for my wife—a wife she only just found out about—probably isn't gaining me any favors. But it's all the truth.

"Fine," Stella scoffs. "We're already in it this deep, so whatever. But you sure as hell aren't leaving me to dig the hole by myself."

"Of course not," I say, relieved. "I can definitely do

that." I mean that, too. That part doesn't seem so intimate. So personal.

Stella rolls her eyes and lets out a long sigh. "Then do something useful, like grabbing some shovels, and start digging," she orders me.

I don't mind her uppity tone for now, because we're getting the job done and she's really doing me a solid on this. So, I get up and leave her to Emily's body. Not only do I not have to move my wife, but I also don't have to watch as her lifeless body is shoved onto the tarp and wrapped up. I hadn't even thought about what that would look like, or how it would affect me, seeing it.

Instead, I will gladly search the property for some shovels.

And that's when I come across the next problem.

I don't see any shovels. None at all. Not even any sort of yard tool like a rake, a hoe, hedge clippers, or even a weed whacker. Not that any of those would do any good, but seriously, there's not a single thing that comes close to being able to dig a hole.

I hear the sounds of Emily's body being rolled onto the tarp as I scour the entire yard. Nothing by the pile of firewood. Nothing but chairs and a rickety fire pit in the center, and nothing around the hole in the fence, where the ladder no longer covers it.

I rush inside the cabin, running up and down the stairs, in and out of the rooms, and yet I still can't find anything. The only place that could even hold any tools is the laundry room, and I find nothing there except some spare light bulbs.

The best thing I can find on the entire property is the tiny shovel for ashes by the wood-burning stove. It's about three inches wide and a half-inch deep at best. There's no way this thing could even break ground, and if it does, then what? Spend a week digging a hole big enough for a body?

I don't think so.

I head back out to see that Stella has finished wrapping my wife in the tarp. I lick my lips, not wanting to tell her. Only a moment ago, I thought I was the one in control, and now it feels like I'm reporting bad news to my boss. What a reversal this has been.

"Find them?" she asks me, wiping her hands together to get the dirt off.

I shake my head. "Nothing," I say, but I have a plan this time. I'm not going to Stella empty-handed, leaving her to figure out yet another step in this process. "I have to go into town to buy some."

The only problem is, do I trust Stella enough to leave her alone with Emily's body? Or do we both go and leave Emily's body behind, out here for anyone who might come by?

FOURTEEN

I drive down the road, checking out the few cabins I can while I pass them on the way to the highway. On the way up here, they felt far more far apart than they do now. All I can think is how cramped they seem now, even though they are more than likely nowhere near as close as the homes down in the valley.

The paranoia is real, but I'd rather that than not be cautious enough.

Which is exactly why I think Stella decided to come along with me. She's quiet as we drive, letting her body move along with each bump of the road, but she doesn't have to say anything for me to know why she came. As worried as I was about leaving her behind with the body, she was even more worried about me leaving her alone with it.

I might have laid it on a little thick when I reminded her that the cabin reservation was in her name, which would look pretty bad to the police. Honestly, I hadn't made up my mind if I should bring Stella with me or leave her there with Emily's body. But

I didn't have to decide because Stella made it a point to come with me.

Is there anything to be gained from that? Could I somehow break away and leave the girl with my wife's body? If I did that, what would I do next? Stella would figure it out soon enough, so I'd have to stay one step ahead of her. And that means I need to call the police first. Maybe I could tell them that Emily went missing, that she thought I was cheating on her when I wasn't because Stella mistook my flirting for an invitation and became obsessed with me.

So obsessed that she rented out a cabin and invited me to join her there. But really, it was all to lure Emily up there. Of course, I would just *speculate* on that part.

But that would work, wouldn't it? I mean, I did make it a point to pay cash for everything.

Plus, Stella did put the rental in her name.

And now that I think of it, I haven't touched Emily's body once since being up here.

At this point, all evidence would point to Stella. Maybe I would need to wipe my fingerprints off a doorknob or two, but other than that, I didn't think there was much to connect me to even being here. Sure, my car is here, but it can easily *not* be here when the police arrive.

How would I explain how Stella got up here? Who cares, that's not my problem. Stella could have hitched a ride for all I know. That's what the police would think, too.

Of course, Stella would turn on me, which is to be expected. But at that point, it's my word against hers. And with no evidence linking me to this crime, the police have no choice but to believe me.

Stella may be pissed at me for lying to her, but this would be far worse. Could I do something like that to someone who is totally innocent in all of this?

That's a question I don't even want to answer, but I may have to down the line. Right now, though, I've been in my head too long.

"Are you gonna turn?" Stella asks, her patience with me already at zero. I've been sitting here at the stop sign, idling away as I think about stabbing Stella in the back. I swallow, a little frightened at where my thoughts have taken me, and try to pull myself back into reality.

"Sorry," I say, turning onto the main highway.

"Everything alright?" she asks me, a hint of suspicion lacing her words. Or maybe I'm just being even more paranoid, feeling like I've been caught doing something wrong. But I feel wrong just thinking about setting her up.

"Yeah. Just thinking about what all we need to buy," I lie.

"I think a couple of shovels and some gloves might do it," she says tersely. "Think they'll have an AC unit that matches?"

I tilt my head in consideration. "Good idea. We can check." Stella has been on top of this whole thing from the start, so maybe trying to turn it around on her isn't the best idea. For now, I'll just keep it in my back pocket in case of an emergency.

The hardware store is up ahead on the left, and I can see its bright red sign glowing as the sun sets. It's nearly dark, so we need to hurry if we want to have any light to bury the body. Of course, digging in the dark will probably be better than in the day, as long as we can do it quietly.

"Let's put flashlights on the list, too," I say, unsure if the cabin has any, but I'd rather be over-prepared than have to make another trip.

Stella doesn't answer me. Instead, she stares intently at the building as we approach the parking lot. Her brows are furrowed like she's trying to see more detail, or like she's trying to interpret something. Maybe it's both.

The parking lot is practically a ghost town. Nobody comes in and out of the store, and there's not a single car parked in the lot. Maybe it's just not a busy time to visit the store.

But it's Stella who puts it together before I do.

"You've got to be kidding me," she says, leaning so far forward, she looks like she's about to climb over the dashboard and through the windshield.

Not only are there no patrons at the store, but there are no employees or their vehicles around the back once I pull further into the lot and can see around the building. I pull up to the front of the store and take the parking spot right in line with the door. It's a handicap spot, but by the looks of things, I don't think anyone will mind.

That's when both of us see the hours of the store.

8 AM - 5 PM

In the top corner of the window, I spot an open sign, but it isn't lit up. My eyes dart down to the clock on the vehicle's center console.

5:49 PM

"Of course." Stella sighs, now that it has been confirmed.

The store is closed.

I don't even know what to say at this point, so I just blurt the question on my mind. It's not even necessarily directed to Stella, but more about my sheer disbelief of the situation.

"What do we do now?"

"We can go back to Payson. Maybe there's another town like Taylor or Holbrook that has someplace open," she says. "I'll look it up."

She pulls her phone out, so I do the same. If we both look, we might be able to find a solution faster. But when I pull up my browser, nothing happens. I watch the spinning wheel and nothing loads. Then I see I have no service.

"I've got nothing," I say, dumbfounded.

"Same here," she says with another sigh.

"By the time we make it to another town, and if we can even find another hardware store, what are the odds you think it'll be open?" I ask.

Stella nods, seeing my point. "Probably close to none."

"We're gonna have to wait till morning," I say. It's the best answer I can come up with, but I wish it weren't the case.

"What if—"

"What?" I cut her off impatiently. "You wanna go door to door and ask people to borrow their shovels? They don't know us. If they live here full-time, they'll probably know the owner of the cabin and wonder why we need to be digging up their yard if we ask for shovels. Best case, they ask a bunch of questions and tell the owner. Worst case, they come by, see what we're up to, and call the cops." I give her a hard look. "You see it going any other way?"

Stella shakes her head, offering up no other solution.

At least this time, I'm the one with the answer, even if I don't like it.

FIFTEEN

It's halfway to the cabin that both of our stomachs growl in unison. All the work of coming up with a solution to cover up a dead body apparently takes its toll. To be honest, I didn't think I'd be hungry at a time like this. But now that I know there's no work to be done until the morning, it's like my body knows it needs to refuel, even in such a stressful state.

As much as my mind wants to ignore the hunger, I also know if we don't eat, we'll regret it tomorrow when we're halfway in the ground, digging a hole.

There were a few places we drove by on the way to the hardware store, but I've never been here, and there are no restaurants I'm familiar with. I don't know if Stella researched the area beforehand or not, but if it were me doing the booking, I would have.

"What do you say?" I ask her. "Think you can eat something?"

Stella nods. "I didn't want to come off as insensitive, but I'm starving," she says.

I smile, knowing exactly what she means. It's nice to see

that she's still basically herself, and that she feels she can be a little open and honest with me right now, even if it's just a small thing like being worried about seeming insensitive.

"Good. I think I saw a place on the way in," I say, zero confidence backing my words. "Unless you have a better suggestion."

"If you flip around, there's a place close to the opposite edge of town."

"Opposite edge of town?" I ask. It seems far when she puts it like that, and she must know what I'm getting at because she has an answer.

"Don't worry, it's not far. Maybe a mile at most," she says. "The town portion is small. It's the trails and woods surrounding it that are big."

"Good to know," I answer. Apparently, she had done her research before coming here.

I find a spot where the road is wide enough and make a U-turn so I'm headed back in the direction of the hardware store. I pass it and find some old-timey buildings up ahead.

"It's over here," Stella says, motioning to the right.

"Wild Women Saloon," I say, reading the building's sign. "I think I've had enough wild for one day."

The joke lands flat with Stella, and I don't blame her. But between my dead wife and talking Stella down from calling the police, at least I didn't say I had enough *wild women* for one day. I'm sure that would have landed more than just flat.

It isn't too busy at the bar right now, with the sun dipping far enough down that I'm sure we only have another fifteen minutes or so of daylight. It's then that it really hits me that we will have to sleep tonight with my wife's body outside in a tarp. I don't really think someone is going to come by to unwrap her, but the fact that she's still out in the open is something that will keep me awake all night.

At least I'll be able to eat, I think to myself as I pull into the parking lot. Not too many cars are here, which is a good thing. The fewer people to see me around town, the fewer people to identify me if anything were to be discovered. Plus, it means we won't have a long wait for our dinner.

Though the building's exterior looks straight out of the Old West, the inside doesn't hold up as well to that theme. It's a bar, sure, with wooden tables and stools, but there's a television in the corner and a pool table to the far left. It's actually quite nice inside, which makes me hopeful that we'll get something good to eat.

"Just sit wherever you like," the waitress calls to us from behind the bar as she loads up drinks on a tray. She's pretty, with curly brown hair, maybe in her mid-fifties.

There's a table right next to the door that both Stella and I gravitate towards. Maybe it's because it's the path of least resistance, or maybe we're just exhausted and want to sit, or maybe we want to be close to the door so we can run if need be. Honestly, any of those things are possible, but neither of us seems to want to discuss why this table seems best. We just sit down at it without a word.

I look to Stella, who seems to be slinking down in her chair, acting like she doesn't want to be spotted. If anything, she looks more suspicious now. I reach across the table and grab her hands. To my delight, she doesn't pull away. She just looks down at them, confused, and back up to me.

"It's gonna be okay," I say. The woman who only moments ago didn't want to seem insensitive by asking to eat is now plagued with worry. I can see it in her eyes.

"How?" she asks. "We are out at a restaurant getting dinner while your wife's dead body is laying in the backyard of a place we rented for the weekend." Her voice is a harsh whisper, and I worry her heated emotions will make it escalate into a yell soon.

I squeeze her hands a little tighter, but gently to show her that I'm here for her. That there is nothing to worry about. Of course, that's not the truth, but I can pretend for her right now. I *need* to. For both of us.

"Right now, we're going to eat, and then we'll go back to the cabin. Nobody knows anything," I say. "I'll be able to fix all of this, alright?"

"Fix this?" she repeats, looking dumbfounded. "How? We have to spend the night in that cabin while she's covered by a tarp just so we can get to an open store and bury her body in the backyard!" Her voice is pushing the limits, and I take a look around to make sure nobody is listening in. "Oh," she adds, "and don't forget that we only have this place until Sunday!"

I want to just tell her to stop, to be quiet, to calm down, but that won't help at all. I can't force her to do anything right now. There's a fine line on what I can do to get her to stop, and I'm not really sure if I can walk it. But I need to figure something out before she has a complete meltdown.

"Everything okay here?" the waitress asks, slowly approaching the table. I was so focused on Stella that I hadn't even noticed the woman come up to us. I take a look at her face, and it's full of concern, but not in a way that tells me she heard anything Stella said. Instead, she gives me a dirty look like I'm the one responsible for upsetting Stella.

I think Stella picks up on it, too, because she nods and meets the woman's gaze. "Yeah, just upset about my grandfather," she says. "He's in hospice right now."

The waitress's face softens. "Oh, hun, I'm sorry. Do you need me to come back or—"

"No, it's okay," Stella says. "Just a tough thing to deal with. We expected this time to come, but I guess no matter how much preparing you do, you just can't fully comprehend until it happens, you know?" To my surprise, a tear drips down her face. She's good. Real good. So much so that I almost start to believe her, too.

"I get it, hun," the waitress says sympathetically.

"We'll go ahead and order now," Stella says, and the waitress has her pen at the ready. "I'll take the chicken-fried steak."

"Great choice," the waitress says. She turns to me, this time without the dirty look.

I didn't even have a chance to look at the menu, so I'm not sure. I don't even know how Stella knew to order a chicken-fried steak, but looking around, it's the kind of place that looks like they sell one. I spot a man at the end of the bar with a pizza in front of him that looks good enough. "I'll take one of those," I say, pointing to the pizza.

The waitress follows my finger and smiles. "Another great choice," she says. She glances around like she's trying to be sneaky and leans in. "You both look like you could use a drink, too, so I'll send over a couple of beers on the house."

She has no idea how true that statement is right now.

We both thank her, and I let out a sigh of relief when she walks away. "Nice job," I say to Stella.

But it's like a switch is flipped, and Stella is no longer in control. She's no longer collected, no longer the calm person who was able to make up a good lie on the fly. Her face twists into worry, and I realize that the pressure put her into focus mode. If she has time to think, then she'll go too far into the abyss. I need to keep her thoughts occupied.

"So, what are you going to do to fix it?" she asks me,

bringing the conversation straight back to where we were before.

The problem is, I don't have an answer. So, I do what any man would do in my position. I stall.

"I need to use the restroom," I say.

Stella grabs my hand, clearly unhappy with the idea of me leaving her. Just like with the trip to the hardware store, she doesn't want to be left behind. Again, I hadn't thought about doing that, and at this point, I still don't want to do that. I just want a moment to myself to collect my thoughts and come up with a plan.

"It's okay," I reassure her, pointing to the bathroom that is plainly in sight of our table. "I'm right there, so you'll see me come out. It's not like I'm going to climb out a window or something." But I immediately regret saying it because now she's thinking it.

"What if—" she starts again.

"Stella, I'll be right back. Look, you can even see the car from here," I say, pointing to the parking lot. My car is right by the front door of the restaurant.

A truck pulls into the lot, but it is too big to park near my car, so it opts for a spot further away from the building where it can fit and not be a bother. When it turns, I see a logo on the side that includes the words LANDSCAPING. In the bed of the truck, I spot a variety of heavy-duty yard tools inside.

And suddenly, I see my next move.

SIXTEEN

The two men from the landscaping truck enter the bathroom shortly after I start washing my hands. From their casual banter, they seem to be in good spirits, not letting a stranger's presence stifle their mood. They're somewhere in their late twenties or early thirties, and from the raggedy condition of their clothes and dirt-caked knees, it looks like they just got off a job.

I had watched them get out of the truck so I could identify them when they sat down. The fact that they came into the bathroom first is just the extra incentive I need. I give them both a nod as they head for the stalls, which they don't seem to notice, and then I dip out of the bathroom before the door can fully close behind them.

Stella catches my eye, but I walk right past our table. I motion for her to stay put, though I'm sure it's going to end up in a long talk, or best-case scenario, she follows me. But much to my surprise, though she scrunches her brow and cocks her head, she listens to me and stays at the table. I wonder if she's seen the landscapers and is on the same wavelength as me.

The sun has now fully set, even though we haven't been here that long. It's far darker here than it is down in the valley. Not many streetlights, save for a few along the highway. There isn't much to light up the parking lot other than the glow from the bar windows and the single bulb at the front door.

That's good for me, because I need the darkness to help me if I'm going to be lurking around the property, trying to steal a couple of shovels.

I exhale, watching my breath unfurl in the air. It's much colder now that the sun has set. A shiver runs through my body. I didn't pack well at all for this trip, but that's not really my top priority right now.

I've never stolen anything in my life, except for a few times at self-checkout, and that was only because I couldn't find the bar code on whatever it was I was trying to buy. If they're gonna make me scan it and bag it, that's where I stop. I'm not gonna chase down an employee to convince them of what the price is or wait while they track it down. So, it just goes in the bag, unscanned. Though I'm not quite the master thief, those times weren't my finest hours, needless to say.

Then again, I'm stealing now for the purpose of burying my dead wife's body, so this is also not my worst hour. Not yet, anyway.

The parking lot is quiet, save for some muffled chatter inside the restaurant. A single car drives down the highway at a speed so fast, they're not trying to get into anyone's business. It's now or never if I'm going to do this. There won't be a better opportunity.

In the bed of the truck, a bunch of different tools are littered about. There's no rhyme or reason for how they've been put inside. I wonder how big of an operation the landscaping business is. It has to be a mess when they get the tools out to start on a job, but that's far from my concern right now.

I spot a dirty shovel lying just next to the wheel well, and I reach in, giving it a tug. But the head of it is stuck under something and won't come out. Gently pulling at the tailgate latch, I release it and bring it down as quietly as possible. But the tailgate has other ideas.

Apparently, not only do these landscapers not keep their tools in good condition, but they don't keep their truck in shape, either. The tailgate brace on the right side doesn't hold, and the entire door pivots on the left side, disconnecting completely from the right side. The tailgate crashes onto the asphalt with a loud *clang*.

I freeze for what feels like an eternity. Did everyone in the bar just hear that noise? Or was it too far away? I think it sounded loud because it's so quiet out here and I'm right next to it. That's what I tell myself, anyway. But I can't help but be overly paranoid and decide that this is not the best place to be. I'll have to scrap this plan and walk away.

"Hey!" I hear a man shout.

They can't be talking to me. I don't even want to look. Spinning around, I start walking in the opposite direction, not even sure where I'm headed other than away from this very spot.

"Hey, I'm talking to you!" he shouts. This time, I'm pretty sure he's shouting at me.

I keep walking, but now, I hear him coming toward me. His footsteps are hard against the pavement, and each time he lifts his feet, I hear bits of gravel scratch against his shoes.

Finally, I turn around to face the man and see that he's just within arm's length of me. It's one of the men I spotted in the bathroom earlier.

"Sorry, I—" I begin.

"Look what he did to your truck, Decon!" His friend, or employee maybe, is by the truck, pointing to the tailgate that dropped to the ground.

"I was just interested in what kind of truck it was," I stammer. "I didn't mean to do any damage. I can pay for it. Maybe I'll buy you guys dinner, too."

"Or maybe we just call the sheriff out here to deal with you," Decon says, glowering at me.

Anything but that, I think to myself. "We don't need to do that," I say placatingly.

"Like hell we don't," Decon growls. He doesn't look like he can be convinced of anything right now. Even in the dark, I can see his face is tinged red.

"It was an honest mistake, guys. Please, I'm sure we can solve this some other way," I say, reaching for my wallet. I have a lot of cash on me since I didn't want to leave a paper trail for Emily to find. There has to be something they'll take.

Decon sneers at me, pulling out his phone. "Like I said, the sheriff can figure it out."

I grit my teeth. This isn't going the way I need it to. "Fine," I say. "Go ahead and call them. I figured you'd need to, anyway. You look the type that has to get the sheriff involved. Can't solve your own problems."

Decon's friend beside the truck stares me down. If Decon isn't taking the bait, this guy sure is. "What'd you say?"

"I said that you and Decon here are too stupid to figure out how to fix your own issues," I say, laying it on thick. "I could have guessed as much from the way you look, so my bad for thinking otherwise. I'm sure you had to get your mom involved in all your fights growing up, too, didn't you?"

Decon's friend holds his stare on me, but this time, he's moving his feet, too. Headed straight for me. "I definitely don't need the cops to solve this problem," he says.

I'm no fighter; that I know well. But it's easier to piss these guys off enough to steer them away from the police. Of course, avoiding a fight is my issue now, but it's a better one than talking to the cops.

To my surprise, it's Decon who steps in. He turns around and plants a hand on his friend's chest. "Not worth it, Max," he says. "You're on probation as it is."

Max meets Decon's eyes, and he stills.

"On probation and still want to call the police?" I ask Max. "You make some friends after your arrest?"

Decon spins around, fire in his eyes, and his fist meets my face before I realize what's even happening. I spin around, seeing the world around me in a quick second, and steady myself. My jaw throbs in pain, but that's okay because soon, I forget all about it when another fist comes at me.

I hear obscenities thrown my way, but I can't tell if it's Decon or Max or both of them. Suddenly, I'm on the ground, feeling the broken asphalt against my cheek as my body continues to take a beating. I think they kick me a few times, too, but it all feels like one big painful experience. Maybe it's for the better that I can't even tell where I'm being hit.

At some point, I close my eyes, but manage to open them again. That's when I spot Stella open the door and gasp.

"Oh my—stop it! Help!" she yells out.

Behind her is a woman I didn't see earlier, but from her apron, she must work at the bar. "I'm calling the sheriff right now!" she yells.

You've got to be kidding me. The whole point was to avoid that. But at least the beating stops.

The men load up into the truck and back out, speeding off before I can tell what direction they're even heading.

Stella runs up to me and crouches down. "Joel. Oh my gosh," she says. It must be bad, but I wonder if it's even worse than I feel. I sure hope not because I can't imagine what that looks like.

"We need to leave," I whisper to her, my mouth filled with the coppery taste of pennies. "We can't be here when the cops show up."

She helps me up, and I see the waitress has the phone to her ear. "You guys stay put," she says. "I'm calling for help."

I wave at her, but decide to not say anything. It would probably look even more suspicious to protest. Instead, Stella and I just get into my car and speed out without a word.

SEVENTEEN

"What the hell were you even thinking?" Stella asks me while I sit in the small bathtub back at the cabin. The water is hot and feels wonderful against my swollen muscles and bruises. She wipes my face with a washcloth since I can barely move right now. I notice the material is crimson with blood when she pulls it away.

"I was thinking we needed some shovels to make this problem go away," I answer, my words slurred from the fat lip that developed on the drive back here.

"That doesn't explain this," she says, motioning to my battered and bruised body in front of her. Even though we've had sex, I would normally feel self-conscious being this naked and vulnerable in front of someone I've been dating for such a short time. But I'm in so much pain right now that I can't care.

"They were going to call the police," I say.

"So what?"

"So if they did that, I'd be arrested, taken in, and then there would be—" I stop myself, but Stella finishes it for me.

"There'd be a record that you were up here," she says,

her voice defeated. "And if that happened, you'd be tied to your wife's location."

I sink lower in the tub, hanging my head. She's not wrong about it, but it's also not the only reason. "I also wouldn't be able to help cover it up," I say, though it sounds so pathetic, I wouldn't believe it myself if I heard it. "And if I were arrested, they might even come to this place to investigate or something." Okay, that one is total crap. Since when does someone get arrested for attempted theft and the police come to search their home with no evidence of anything else stolen? Never, that's when.

But Stella doesn't seem to notice. Instead, she just continues to wipe the blood off my face, her hands still soft and gentle as she does it.

"I'm sorry," I say finally. This time, I think it's believable. It better be, because I actually mean it. "After all I've done to you, I don't deserve you still taking care of me like this." I feel water roll down my cheek, but I think it's a tear. "I'm not a good person, am I?"

I look up at Stella's face and see no signs of anger anymore. Instead, it's filled with pity. I don't think I deserve pity, either, but I'll take it. I know if I weren't cheating, then I wouldn't be in this place to begin with. My wife would have had no reason to look for me, and she'd be alive. I'd be at home, enjoying my life. Not messing the whole thing up.

But it's too late for any of that now.

I keep looking at Stella, hoping for an answer. Hoping to be let off the hook. But I know it's not her responsibility to do that. Still, she does it, anyway.

"It's okay," Stella says, her eyes kind. "I doubt I'm any better."

"What do you mean?" I ask, frowning in confusion. The only thing she's done wrong is believe me. She thought I was single; she wanted to call the police. Maybe she feels bad about following along with my plan to bury Emily, which is one more reason for me to feel guilty. But it's for the best. That, I'm sure of.

She smiles and holds a hand out to me. "Come on, let's get you upstairs into bed," she says.

I let her help me up and dry me off. She was even thoughtful enough to have my pajamas out and ready for me to step into them, and had the wood-burning stove going so that the cabin is nice and toasty when I emerge from the bathroom.

She hands me a warm mug with cinnamon wafting from it. It's some sort of tea, which isn't my usual, but she gives me an encouraging look. "Go ahead, it'll help soothe your aches. It's my grandmother's recipe. It's also great for bedtime, so I don't go anywhere without it."

I take a long swig of it. The flavors are subtle but tasty. The warmth fills me from the inside, and I drink it all down as fast as I can to make Stella happy, and so I can get to bed. I doubt I'll sleep much, but I'll try anything at this point. I hand her the mug when I'm finished.

The bed is warm once I make my way up the stairs and into it. My body aches, but I'm hoping that in the morning, I won't be in so much pain. I have a lot to do, after all. "Thank you," I say to Stella. Even though it's warm in the bed and the fire has heated up the whole cabin, I still feel a shiver run across me. I am greedy for rest, but still worried it won't come.

"We're in this together," she says. "Even if you lied, well, I still don't want to see you hurt like this."

I smile, powering through the pain. Stella is more mature than I would have given her credit for, and she's definitely a better person than I am. "You're a good person,"

I say, telling her what I'm thinking. "What did you mean when you said you weren't any better?"

Already, I'm feeling pleasantly groggy. I'll have to find out the recipe for that tea because I could use it on a daily basis. It's also possible that I'm just that exhausted.

"I guess I thought this was my restart," Stella says, but I can tell there's more. I stare at her, waiting. She tucks a strand of hair behind her ear. "My ex wasn't the greatest guy. But still, I might have taken it too far when things ended."

I'm struggling to keep my eyes open, and her words are distant.

"I'm sure you have nothing to worry about," I say, my own words sounding so far away, like I'm not even the one saying them. Am I even having a conversation right now?

"The things I've done in my past," she says, sounding further and further away. "Everything people have said about me, they just..."

After that, her words become a low hum, and I can't make anything out. My eyes are closed, and I'm drifting off to the sound of her voice as she keeps speaking to me. Something about her being here puts me at ease, even though I should be anything but. It's like Stella has always been a part of me, something I can't even put into words. I'm not making much sense right now, but I know there has to be something there.

And that's the last thing I think of before I'm completely out.

EIGHTEEN

Stella

I know Joel has lied to me, and somehow, he's convinced me not to call the police. He didn't outright threaten me, but I sensed some sort of implication in his words to me. Still, I made my choice, and this is what we're doing. Too late to back away from it now, right?

So, yes, Joel might be a scumbag, but he does just regular scumbag things. Aren't most guys that way? He cheated on his wife, lied to me, wants to cover up the accident and bury a body—alright, that one is outside the realm of *normal* scumbag material—but still, is he all *that* bad?

Joel is a liar and a cheater, so maybe he deserved to get his ass handed to him in the parking lot. But that's it. All this other stuff, his wife being dead and him having to bury her, he doesn't deserve all that. Just a moment ago, he was remorseful, reflecting on what led him to this moment. He feels emotion like most everyone does.

And yet, we're still in this pickle, aren't we? An accident Joel doesn't want to call in, and I have a feeling there is something else he's not telling me. More than just something as simple as him being married. How funny to call that "simple," but it's true. The way he's been acting, the way he doesn't want to call in his wife's death as an accident. And then there's that little pull inside me that thinks that name he let slip—Angela—relates to more than he let on.

And then, there are my own secrets.

I nearly just let everything slip out because I feel bad for Joel. Luckily, he fell asleep, and I don't think he heard everything. That's for the best, though. I know it. And as much as I want to get everything off my chest, Joel discovering my secrets would make him turn on me. Hell, if he found out *everything* about me, then I'm sure he would do more than just turn. It would break him, and I don't know if he could ever recover.

The truth is, I can't have the police sniffing around me, either. And there's no way in hell I can tell Joel that because, like I said, it wouldn't be good for either of us. So, it's best to just go along with the plan right now. I knew that the moment I started to go along with it. There was no turning back.

It's far too late to deviate. Once the plan started, the only way out is through to the end.

NINETEEN

Joel

I feel like I'm floating, but not in a light, airy way. No, this doesn't feel good at all. It feels like a rush of blood, making me light-headed and unsure where I am. I'm overstimulated, with my anxiety off the charts, while at the same time, I'm so groggy that I don't want to open my eyes.

In a way, it's like I'm hung over—or hell, maybe still drunk, though I know I didn't have any alcohol the night before. I only drank that tea. And got a full-blown ass-whooping from those two guys in the parking lot.

Maybe that's why I also feel like I just woke up from surgery. Like the leftover medication is still working its way out of my body, when really, it was because of all that happened to me just before passing out.

I know what I have to do today, but I still can't bring myself to open my eyes. I feel the sunlight on my face; we didn't pull down the curtains over the window where the air conditioner once was. The sun is warm on my skin, which is quite nice because I'm still sore. I'm reminded of what happened once I wriggle to a sitting position that will help me fully wake up.

I reach over, but feel nothing beside me in the bed. In fact, the spot where I assumed Stella slept is cold. I slept like a rock—how, I'm not sure, exactly—but it seems she's been awake for a while. Stress affects people in different ways, I guess.

It's not even Stella's absence that makes me stir, but the sound of her voice. Because she clearly isn't in the same room as me, or even downstairs calling out to me. It sounds like she's outside, her voice drifting up through the crack in the window, and she certainly isn't talking to me.

But she is talking to someone.

I open my eyes fully, and immediately regret that decision. The sun is blaring through the window, and I shield my eyes as best I can with my hand. It takes a minute before I can adjust to the light, but it settles enough that I can finally peer through the window.

But I don't see anything. I only see the open backyard, where I need to dig a hole to put my dead wife's body in and cover it back up.

I don't hear any more talking, either. I start to question if I ever did in the first place.

The front door opens, and the air changes throughout the whole house. "Joel?" Stella calls out after shutting the door. "You awake yet?"

"Yeah," I call back, my voice weak and scratchy. I clear my throat. "Up here, still in bed."

Her footsteps are loud and purposeful as she climbs the stairs. I worry she's upset about something—well, something new that I'm not privy to yet. But when I see her face, she doesn't seem any more irritated than she was the day before. I will consider that a win at this point.

"What were you doing out there?" I ask. She's already dressed for the day, wearing something nice. Not anything I would consider appropriate for yard work.

Yard work...is that all this is to me now? Whatever the case, Stella doesn't look like she's about to start digging in the dirt.

Then again, what did I pack that would be appropriate for that task? Nothing, that's what. Neither one of us planned for this day.

"Just getting some fresh air," she says. "Seeing what the weather is like."

"I thought I heard you talking outside," I say.

She gives me an odd look at first, but then realization sets in and she relaxes. "I sometimes talk to myself. It's like when I am nervous about doing something like—"

"Right," I interrupt, sparing her from having to say "bury a body".

"If I can just talk myself through it first, then I will realize it's easy enough and I'm not blowing anything out of proportion," she says. "Even if the truth might be otherwise."

It all makes sense to me, and I didn't want to be paranoid with her. It's not like she was out there talking to some neighbor about burying the body, right? If that were the case, I'm sure the police would be here by now.

I guess I'm just nervous about all of it, too. Maybe talking myself through it would do me some good.

"Whatever was in that tea worked a miracle," I say, changing the subject. "I can see why you drink that every night. Didn't work for you last night, though?"

She shrugs. "After I made the cup for you and helped

you into bed, I was exhausted and didn't think I needed it. Bad choice, though, because I woke up in the middle of the night and couldn't fall back to sleep. Nerves, I guess."

I nod. "I'm sorry you had to help me," I say truthfully.

She shakes her head like it's not a big deal. "How are you feeling?" she asks, her turn to change the subject.

I cock my head. I could lie and say that I'm feeling like a spring chicken, but it would be far too obvious that I'm not, especially considering that I haven't even gotten out of bed, and every time I move, I wince at the aches in my body. Nothing I can't deal with, but nothing I need to lie about, either. "Maybe a little better than a bag of ass, but it's iffy," I say, trying to keep the mood light.

It seems to work, because I catch a small smile from Stella. Maybe I still have a way to charm her, not that I'm trying for anything more than keeping us as happy as possible, considering what we're dealing with. I'll take it for now.

"Not sure about you, but I could use something to eat," she says.

I nod. "Same. But maybe there's a drive-thru or a pickup window where we can just grab something. I'd like to avoid any sit-downs after last night." I rub my face, feeling the swelling there.

She agrees. "Get dressed. The hardware store is going to be open in fifteen minutes, so we've got time to figure it out."

TWENTY

I try to scarf down an omelette while I drive. Stella pointed out a pickup window at some little café whose name I didn't catch. I didn't even care because the smells coming out of the place were divine. And this omelet is solid. If only I could figure out how to steer and use a fork at the same time without sending us crashing into oncoming traffic. I've only had a couple of bites, but hope to eat more when we park.

The hardware store is far busier today than yesterday, which is good, considering it was closed when we were last here. There's a spot only a few places away from the door that opens up when a large truck backs out and exits the parking lot.

I swoop in, throwing the car into park. I carefully study the entrance, watching an older man walk out with his hands full of paint supplies. Looking through the glass doors, I can make out some employee walking by with his red vest on. I'm glad the store is open, but it's almost too busy for my liking.

Stella must be thinking the same thing because I spot

her biting her bottom lip like she's nervous or unsure. She turns to me and takes a good look at my face.

"Maybe you should stay here and let me buy everything," she offers.

"You sure?" I ask.

"With the way you look right now, you might just bring more attention," she says. "And then you can finish your breakfast. It makes the most sense."

She's not wrong, but I feel like I should object, anyway. Something about the man needing to buy the tools or something, as stupid as it sounds. I don't want her having to do everything...but it would be nice to just eat my eggs right now.

"I think I'll be okay," I say, though I don't mean it.

"No, I'm doing it," she insists, holding her hand out. "Do you have any cash on you?"

I fish out my wallet and put the money in her hand. It's enough to buy everything we need and then some. "You know what to get, right?"

"We talked about it last night," she reminds me.

"Right," I say.

She steps out of the car, but lingers halfway inside. I can tell something is on her mind. She turns to me hesitantly. "Can I get the keys, too?"

I snicker, the idea of driving off not even crossing my mind this time. But I don't blame her for asking. I pull the car keys out and slap them in her hand, not aggressively, but in a way I hope conveys I have no inclination of bailing. "Of course," I say. "I'll be right here eating my omelette when you get back."

She gives me a painful smile. "Sorry."

I want to tell her not to be. That yesterday, I was an asshole who had been considering taking off on her. But there's no need for that now. And it's not even on my mind to do it after she took care of me last night.

We're in this together. I really feel this way now.

Anything I can do to help Stella trust me at this point, I will do it. I've given her plenty to not trust me with, so it's the least I can do.

I watch as she walks away from the car and into the store. The door closes, and I lose sight of her. She shouldn't be too long, but just long enough for me to finish this delicious omelette. I quickly open the container and shovel the food into my mouth as if I haven't eaten in a week. In only a few minutes, the whole thing is gone.

I lean back in my seat, still very tired. I let out a loud belch, grateful that I'm alone in the car, and watch people go in and out of the store. I toss the food container in the backseat, over the idea of keeping a clean car, and figure I can throw out any trash when this is all behind me. Having a messy car is at the bottom of my list of priorities right now.

For such a small town, the hardware store is far busier than I would have expected. Cars continue to pull up at the same rate other vehicles pull out. It's like it's the hub of the area and everyone uses this place. That is probably a lot closer to the truth than I realize. It's so different from where I live in the valley. I don't even live downtown, but in a suburb of Phoenix. It feels so less connected down there than here, and I almost wish I had something like this, where I could randomly bump into neighbors and chat.

Of course, I can't do that in light of my current predicament. I'm more than grateful that I don't know any of these people. Otherwise, I'm sure they'd all be up in my business.

I slink down in the seat, watching the people come and go, and then I feel the weight of my eyelids. I'm still so tired and could use a little rest. I close my eyes, knowing I won't have a chance to get a whole lot of sleep. But just enough of a recharge until Stella gets back, maybe. A few minutes of just collecting myself is all I need.

And then I hear a man shouting.

I open my eyes and see it's been almost ten minutes since I shut them, according to the clock. I would be more impressed with the lost time if Stella wasn't the person this man was yelling at.

She carries a variety of tools in her hands, bundled close to her. The man is thick-waisted, with a beard that stretches down until it touches his chest. He is scary-looking to me, made even more frightening by the way he's yelling at Stella, who looks so tiny next to him.

At first, my stomach drops, thinking that she stole those items. But then I spot the receipt in her hand that flutters in the breeze. I have no idea what the issue is, but from how fast Stella is walking, it's clear she doesn't want to hang around to find out.

I reach for the door handle, ready to get out and shout back at the man. Some sort of defense seems necessary in this situation. And as much as I don't want to have to fight him, with last night's experience still fresh in my mind, I feel like I need to get involved.

But Stella meets my gaze as she strides toward me, giving me a single shake of her head. She motions with her chin to the car, and I catch her meaning. I pop the trunk open, and she makes a beeline straight for it, dumping the tools and supplies inside. The weight of the car shifts as she slams the trunk door back down.

She rushes toward the passenger seat and slides in after opening the door, tossing me the keys all in one fluid motion.

"Drive," she says.

The belligerent man starts toward us, and I don't hesitate to start the car up. I watch as he twists his face, almost like it's in disgust. I never heard what he was saying, even though he was very loud.

"What is that guy's problem?" I ask Stella.

"Let's just go," she says, this time in a more pleading tone.

Hitting the gas, I pull out of the parking spot and drive straight out of the lot. I keep an eye on the man who accosted Stella in the rearview mirror, but he doesn't seem interested in taking down my plate number. He just watches us leave.

TWENTY-ONE

Once the car is unloaded, I decide it's better to pull it out of the driveway and park it down the street a little ways. I'm being paranoid again, but Stella agrees with me. Better to look like nobody is here so some friendly neighbor doesn't get the idea to come greet us while randomly driving by.

I have no idea how to go about finding the best spot to bury a body in the yard, so I just pick a place, somewhat tucked against the back wall, but not too close so that anyone who lives nearby might hear or get suspicious. We've already started digging, and now that I'm looking at it, I worry it's too close to the center.

Of course, would I be happy with anywhere I picked? I'd be nitpicking it to death, constantly worrying about who might dig into it and for what reasons. Would they want to do some landscaping? Plant some trees? Maybe they'd want to lay down pavers? Hell, what if they decide to dig an entire pool here?

All these thoughts run through my head, but I try to keep them at bay. There will never be a perfect solution, so

I just have to do the best I can. If I keep second-guessing myself, I'll never get anywhere.

And we have to leave tomorrow. Some other poor soul might be up here to rent, and I can't have them come across us still digging up the place. I wonder if their trip will be as messed up as ours is now.

We are maybe a foot into the ground now, but the hole is nowhere near as wide as we need it to be. Whenever they show people digging up a grave on TV, it takes up fifteen seconds of screen time. But to my disappointment, we've been digging for an hour, and it feels like this is going to take all day. And that's if we're lucky.

I hope to god we are, because so far on this trip, we've been anything but lucky.

I look by the window, where Emily's body is still wrapped in the tarp. It's been untouched since Stella rolled her up in it, which is a relief. I can't even see Emily's body inside it, but if I saw it had been moved from where we last put it, I'd be freaking out right now. The last thing I need is to wonder if someone's been rummaging around the property and found her body. I swallow down that idea, telling myself those thoughts will end up nowhere good, and get back to digging.

Turning my attention back to Stella seems to be the best course of action.

"What happened at the hardware store?" I finally ask, never getting a direct answer from her about that whole ordeal. She hadn't felt the need to talk about it. Besides, it seemed like getting to work on this little *project* was more pertinent than some random encounter at the store.

Stella shakes her head, digging at the sides to widen the hole. "Some asshole," she says, not elaborating.

I keep at the hole, digging deeper into the ground,

tossing the shovelfuls of dirt to the side where a pile is building. "That's it? He seemed pretty upset about something."

"He asked for my number, but I told him I wasn't interested," she says. "Guy wouldn't take a hint, I guess."

I stop digging and watch her. I don't know why she's not angrier about it. Sure, digging this grave is probably more important, but shouldn't she be pissed about the guy? "Seems a little excessive over a phone number," I remark. I don't mean to come off as condescending or suspicious, but even I can admit I sound that way.

She stops digging and stares at me. So much for the goodwill and pity I've earned from her. Now she looks like she wants to strangle me instead of soothe me.

"You have no idea what it's like to be a woman, Joel," she says, firing her words like an automatic rifle. "Some men think they're entitled to my attention. They tell me to smile, they tell me to be polite, they tell me to take a joke, they tell, they tell, they tell. But if the tables were turned and *I* were to tell them what to do, I'd be labeled a bitch, or worse. So, yes, Joel, it is absolutely excessive over just a phone number, but that's not on me. That's on every asshole who wants to tell me I can't take a joke, who can't take *no* for an answer. That's what it's like to be a woman."

She picks up her shovel, squeezing the handle as tight as possible. If she weren't wearing garden gloves to avoid getting blisters, I'm sure I'd see her knuckles going white as snow.

I watch her carefully as she raises the shovel. I lift mine hesitantly, worried about what she's thinking, what she's about to do. Am I going to have another body on my hands? This time, one of my own doing?

But Stella lets out a long exhale that sounds like a resigned growl and digs her shovel straight into the hard soil. Her eyes quickly go back to the task in front of her, and I let out a sigh of relief as quietly as possible. I don't want her to know just how much she scared me for so many reasons.

I don't know what just happened, but our relationship feels off to me. Stella seems far more unstable than when we first got here. Or, hell, from when I first met her about a month ago.

But a stressful situation like this one can do a lot of things to a person.

What scares me the most, though, is that it's only going to get more stressful from here.

TWENTY-TWO

The hole is halfway there, but it's taking far longer than expected. The day is mostly gone. At this rate, it's going to be dark when we finally get the body into the hole. The cover of darkness might be a good thing, but we've run into no issues digging so far, so it seems like we may not even need it.

Because once the body is in the hole, we still have to cover it back up with all the dirt we just dug up. Of course, that task should be easier, but it still feels like it's going to be an all-night thing.

I don't think I'll be getting any sleep at this point.

After Stella schooled me on what it's like to be a woman, and then almost made me believe she was going to take my head off with a shovel, I figured it was best for us to just work in silence. She must have had the same idea, because we spent the rest of the time digging away, not uttering a single word to each other, only a series of sighs, grunts, and even a couple of *ows* as we strained ourselves. Or, in my case, wasn't paying attention and clipped my foot with the shovel.

That's when I decide to take a break and get some water in the cabin. We both need to rest and rehydrate. Besides, taking a brief moment away from each other might be good for us.

"Need anything?" I ask Stella, hoping this question will warm her to me again. With the tension so high between us, we're one wrong word away from flying off the handle and becoming mortal enemies. I think both of us would like to try to avoid that scenario.

She takes a deep breath, walking toward the cabin and propping her shovel against the siding. "Yeah, if you don't mind bringing out some water, I'd appreciate it. I just want to sit down for a second." There's no animosity lacing her words. Like me, she's just exhausted.

I nod to her as she catches her breath. "Of course, I'd be happy to. You take your time," I say, trying to be as delicate and agreeable as I can lest she find another reason to berate me.

I head into the cabin and am immediately met by cold air. Even though the upstairs air conditioner is gone, the one sitting beside the front door, in the window over the dining table, is blowing at full blast. It makes me realize just how sweaty I am, and I immediately grab at my shirt so the sweat doesn't cling to my skin. I give it a few pumps with my hand, trying to dry it out, though I know it won't amount to much.

The front door doesn't close all the way and rests against the door jamb. I leave it there and head to the restroom before getting water out of the fridge. Even though it feels like I've sweated out gallons of water, I somehow still need to piss.

And as soon as I get to the toilet, the water is not shy about evacuating.

I stand there, letting out a long sigh. I haven't had a moment to just be still and alone. And I'm almost put at ease in this small moment of relief, of course, until I hear the engine of a car and tires crunching over the gravel just outside. I quickly give two shakes and flush the toilet as I rush to the window to see who is driving up.

Immediately, I'm plagued with frantic thoughts of who it could be. Is it that guy from the hardware store? Did he somehow find out where we were staying? And if so, what does he really want? Or maybe it's worse, and it's those two guys from last night, the ones I tried to steal from. Did they come to have another go at me? And what for? I mean, I did damage their truck, but still, that's pretty ballsy because I would have all the more reason to call the police on them now.

When I finally look out the window, I see it's a new person. But that doesn't bring me relief. In fact, this person is far, far worse than I imagined.

Because pulling up to our little driveway is a car with lights on top and a star emblem on the side.

The sheriff is here for us.

TWENTY-THREE

Stella

Is that really a car pulling around the cabin right now? Maybe it's just passing by, looking for their rental. Clearly, it's not uncommon around here. But then why does it sound like it's pulling up to the house and into the driveway?

I know it's not Joel since he made it a point to not park in the driveway, but instead, down the road. Even if he had parked in the driveway, why would he invest all this time and bail now?

At this point, I think Joel is in this with me. Which is good, because I'd be totally screwed without him as part of this plan.

I spring up from the plastic Adirondack chair I had dragged into the shade near the cabin wall and peek through the gap in the slats of the fence.

That's when my stomach drops.

Not only is it a car that's not just passing by, but it's driving directly up to the cabin. To top it all off, it also looks to be a sheriff's vehicle, going by the emblem on the side of the door.

I wipe the sweat from my brow, now from pure stress instead of physical exertion, and squint to see who might be inside the car. The person behind the wheel doesn't look like the sheriff. He's far too young. More than likely a deputy.

He gets out of the car, and I quickly swivel my head around, seeing the state of the backyard. We've dug a big trench in the backyard, and there's still the rolled-up tarp. Thankfully, no body parts can be seen, but the trench still looks awfully suspicious. Body-sized, to be exact. How am I going to explain this?

The deputy steps out. He's fairly good-looking, with his brown hair only slightly disheveled, and wearing a pair of aviator sunglasses. I can tell he's not overweight, but not quite the young, fit stud straight out of a movie or romance novel. He's headed right for the gate, but suddenly stops and turns to the door.

The way Joel handled the last interaction with people, I have zero faith that he can talk his way out of this one. Of course, the deputy had to come right now, when we're in the middle of digging a grave, and now he's going to ruin the whole plan.

I know I have to intervene if we have any chance of getting out of this one. So, I quickly unlatch the gate and step out of the yard with a smile. I try to pull the gate closed behind me, but don't make a big deal about it, knowing the deputy's focus might turn to what I'm doing back there.

"Oh, hello," I say to the deputy, trying to keep it light

and acting surprised to see him. Of course, I *am* surprised to see him, but not in the thanks-for-stopping-by way I pretend to show.

"Hello, miss," he says, his head dipping slightly. His eyes are hidden behind his sunglasses, but I can tell he's giving me a good up-and-down with them. A small smile forms on his lips. Maybe he likes what he sees, though I'm pretty dirty and sweaty. But hey, maybe that's his thing. I'll play up what god gave me right now if that's what it takes to get out of this.

"Can I help you with something?" I ask, eyeing the door jamb and seeing it's not fully latched. I keep my voice louder than normal, hoping Joel can hear me and stay inside. I'm not trying to protect him from being spotted, but the fewer people know we're up here together, the better it is for everyone. Less chance of our story going off the rails. If there is to be a story to be told to anyone after all of this.

It's at the top of my list not to have one to tell after this weekend.

The deputy, who wears a badge on his chest that reads "D. Larson", pulls his full attention on me. He's no longer facing the door, which is a good start. Now I just have to figure out how to get him out of here.

"Just coming by to check out the area," he says. "I do a sweep every so often, that kind of thing." It seems like a normal part of his job, except for the part about ending up in our driveway.

"Is there a problem?" I ask.

"No, not at all," he says, but his body language is still stiff, which doesn't make me feel reassured. "Like I said, just a sweep."

"But you came and stopped by my place here," I say,

careful not to say "our place". That would be a guarantee he'd ask who else is with me.

The deputy smiles for longer than I'd like, seemingly trying to figure me out. Am I being overly suspicious right now? I try to smile, keep it friendly—and pull my shoulders back, hoping my cleavage shows a little more. If it does, he doesn't seem to notice.

"I just saw the door ajar," he says. "Thought I saw some people around, so figured I'd come by. On occasion, we get some calls about a dog on the loose."

"Did you this time?"

He shakes his head. "Nope. But haven't caught one, either. Figured I'd give whoever's here a heads-up just in case. A lot of rentals around here, and most people might not know to keep an eye out."

"Thanks for that," I say with a warm smile. "But so far, so good here." I hope his curiosity is satiated, and he can hurry up out of here.

He leans on one foot as a breeze blows past. I hear the creak of the gate behind me. That's not good at all. I must not have latched it fully when I closed it, and now the breeze has pulled it back open.

"Got some project going on back there?" he asks.

I close my eyes and take a breath for what feels like an eternity but is only a half-second, then glance over my shoulder. The gate is wide open, and I can see straight into the yard, where there is a big hole in the ground next to a large pile of dirt. At the very least, the rolled-up tarp is out of view, but if he gets any more curious and wants to take a step back there, all bets are off.

I've got to be quick.

"Yeah, you could say that," I say, still acting friendly but trying to sound exhausted, too. "Had some septic issues."

He nods, and I can see his eyebrows lift above the rim of his sunglasses. "You own this place?"

"Yes," I say, deciding that there would be no reason for a renter to dig up the backyard. "Just don't make it up here much these days." I don't know if that's overkill, but I figure it might help since he just said he makes a sweep every so often up here. I just hope to god he doesn't ask to see my ID, but I know he has no reason to ask. It would look really suspicious if I told him no.

"A big job for one person," he remarks.

He doesn't know how true that statement is.

"You're not kidding," I say, leaning into it. "Figured I'd save some money and excavate it myself over a week or so. Too much money to rent a backhoe up here, you know?" I hope he does know, because I sure as hell don't.

He nods again. "I'd have asked some friends for help if I were you," he says.

"Oh, I don't have a ton of those up here who don't flake out," I say with a grin.

"I know the feeling on that one," he says, now grinning. I don't catch a whiff of suspicion coming from him now.

"Thanks for stopping by," I say, steering the conversation to an end. "I better get back to it if I want to capitalize on this daylight."

"If you find yourself in a jam and you're still up here, I'm off on Tuesday," he says. "I can swing by and check in, if that's okay with you?" Apparently, my half-assed attempt at flirting did better than I figured.

"Not sure if I'll still be at it, but feel free," I say. I don't really want him sniffing around, but I figure it's better than hurting his feelings. By Tuesday, this should all be over, anyway.

"See you around," he says before turning and getting in

his car. I keep a smile on my face and wave as he pulls out and onto the road, headed in the opposite direction. I keep watching until he is fully out of view and let out a huge sigh of relief.

TWENTY-FOUR

Joel and I waited a good fifteen minutes to get back to work. I made sure he still stayed in the cabin in case the deputy decided to come back. In the meantime, I spent my time pacing around, acting like I was busy, and walked down the road a little ways to see if I could spot the deputy still circling the area.

He never circled back, though, and I never even saw him driving around when I further walked down the road. So he must have bought my story, unless he was just gathering backup to come and sweep the property. But I don't believe that to be the case.

The most that Joel and I exchanged were a few words of relief, plus a knowing glance that told us how close a call that was. The odds of a random deputy driving through, pulling up to our cabin, and telling me about the dog on the loose in the neighborhood were extremely slim, but it still happened, nearly blowing the whole plan.

Even though the deputy had nothing to suspect, just thinking about the exchange leaves me with a racing heart.

Once we felt the coast was clear, there was nothing

more to do than get back to work. I don't know if it was just from the digging together, or maybe our shared fear over the whole deputy thing, but I was no longer upset with Joel. And it didn't seem like he was holding any grudges over my berating him about the guy at the hardware store, either. In fact, he was being even nicer, probably not wanting to reignite whatever fuse he had lit in the first place. But hey, I'll take it. Makes for a more pleasant work environment, and that's what this is right now. Work.

And both of us got straight back into it, resuming our system of digging and not speaking, but mostly just to conserve our energy. On top of that, the idea of digging a grave is not conducive to stirring up a pleasant conversation. Neither of us seemed to mind, though, and we were making quick work.

Well, the work felt quick, but as the sun told us, it wasn't as quick as we wanted. Because now that we've finished digging a deep enough and wide enough hole, the sun is completely past the horizon. Other than the moonlight, we only have the couple of flashlights I managed to pick up at the hardware store.

Joel stands at the edge of the grave while I'm inside it, the ground just above my head. It's kind of creepy, and I can't wait to get out of the thing, so I hold my hand out to him.

I watch Joel's face as he eyes my hand, and I can't help but think how easy it would be for him to just swing the shovel down on me and leave me in here with his wife. The thought of being buried in the backyard gives me the shivers.

But he quickly reaches a hand down, grasping my own, and hoists me up so I can get a good footing and climb out.

Being out of the grave now makes me feel so much better. Thankfully, I won't need to be back in there again.

No, it's reserved for another.

Both of us must be thinking the same thing because we look over to the side of the cabin where the rolled-up tarp still is. But we both know it's more than just a tarp. It's a secret that we have to keep.

Neither one of us says anything about it, though. We both know what we have to do, but neither of us takes the first step.

"That was quick thinking," Joel says. "Earlier, I mean. With the sheriff."

"Deputy," I correct, as if it matters. "But thanks." I offer a smile I'm sure he can't even see.

We both sit in the silence of the night for a moment. I look around at the night sky, the stars twinkling above. It's beautiful up here, and I wish I could enjoy it instead of having this crazy weekend, but I can't go thinking that way now. It's too late, and I've learned that past regrets are nothing but trouble. If I stop to think about them, then I'll never be able to move forward again.

Joel speaks first, breaking the silence once again. "I, uh, I'm not sure..." He swallows, like he can't even bring himself to say whatever he's thinking. But I have a feeling I already know what he's going to ask.

I turn around, now even further from the hole so that I'm between him and the cabin.

"I'm not sure I can stomach pushing her—it, I mean, you know—" He motions to the ground where the blue tarp lays. "Can you do it?"

I stare, blinking in disbelief.

I can't believe it.

"Stella?" Joel asks, but I pay no attention to his words.

Instead, I'm focused on what I'm seeing just over his shoulder.

"Joel," I finally say, with my eyes locked on the spot. "What the hell is that?"

I point at the little red dot, like a laser cutting through the pitch black of night. The little red dot attached to a video camera.

The video camera that's pointed right at us.

TWENTY-FIVE

"I'm telling you, Joel, that's a video camera," I say.

He's squinting in the dark, putting his hand over his eyes like he's shielding them from something, but there's no sun out right now, so I have no idea what he's doing. I don't know if he's just in denial, disbelief, or just plain can't see the thing. But I know what I'm looking at right now, even if he says otherwise.

Which, of course, he continues to do, even now. "I don't know," he says, the confidence in his voice more annoying than anything else right now. It's like he just wants to double down on his stupidity. "I don't think that's what it is. Maybe it's just a security light, you know? One of those things that gets triggered when someone walks by. I think that's what it is. You're just paranoid and overreacting."

I really can't stand when someone tells me how to feel. And right now, Joel is getting on my last nerve. I'm really starting to wonder what I ever saw in him in the first place. Sure, he wasn't my ideal type to begin with, but he charmed the hell out of me early in this relationship.

But now? Honestly, this guy would be lucky if I didn't

just scurry off. Or worse, tell him to leave me the hell alone and convince some bigger, stronger guy to pretend he was my boyfriend so the idiot that is Joel would take the hint.

Unfortunately, we're stuck with each other. For the time being, anyway. After this weekend, however, I doubt either one of us will ever want to see each other again.

"Joel, I'm telling you—"

"And I'm saying—"

"Maybe it's just that you're too old to see it!" I finally say. "Clearly, my eyes work better than yours."

That shuts him up, and I walk to the edge of the yard, right where the fence stops me. The house on the other side is a ways past what I assume is their side of the yard, though they don't have a fence over their property line. I lift my flashlight and shine it right at the red dot, where right next to it, I can see the lens.

The light is too weak to reach all the way to the cabin, at least at full strength, but it gives just enough light that Joel finally gets the picture.

"Holy crap," he says, and I can't help but let a smug smile creep across my face. "Are you sure it's pointing here, though? Maybe it's just at the yard and not all the way to us."

I hang my head and grit my teeth. Joel is really pushing it now. I take a deep breath and turn around to face him. He's headed toward me to get a better look himself.

"I'm not sure, Joel," I say wryly. "Neither one of us noticed it before, but here we are. Maybe it can't see us, and if that's the case, then great. But here's a question, so maybe you can play along with me for a minute, okay? What if it can see us? How will we know for sure one way or the other? Are you willing to take that chance? Because I know my answer to that." I'm laying it on thick, and I hope he feels like a complete idiot right now. I hope he catches my smugness and patronizing tone. I am absolutely talking down to him right now, and I want him to know it.

Don't treat me like I don't know what I'm talking about. I will always come back and win that game. I'll make sure of it, one way or another. Sometimes to my detriment.

I've burned far too many bridges that way.

But in the end, I showed them, didn't I?

Joel doesn't say much, which means he's taking his lumps like I hoped he would. Now, maybe we can actually figure this thing out together.

"Sorry," he says, which makes me feel good and vindicated. "You're right." Again, vindicated.

"So what should we do?" I ask.

"We need to get a better look," he says. "Let's head around and take a look, don't you think?"

"Yeah, okay, but what about after that?" I press. "We can look and debate all we want, but if that thing is pointing right at us while we're burying your dead wife, not a whole lot is going to be gained from getting a better look." I might have been a little harsh on that one, but it feels like a bit of a pickle at this point. "So what then?"

"I know," Joel says with a sigh. "We're gonna have to break in and delete the footage."

TWENTY-SIX

Joel

I don't really know what I was thinking when I said we would have to break in and delete the footage. I mean, I know exactly what I meant, but I didn't quite know what that would entail. After all, I've never broken into someone's house, never looked for video files, and never deleted them off someone's hard drive like I'm some secret agent.

Then again, I've never had to dig a grave, cover up an accidental death, and bury a body until now. I guess this whole weekend is full of firsts for me. What a great learning experience.

My sarcasm knows no bounds when I'm in my own thoughts.

Stella helps me navigate in the darkness with her flashlight. The ground is uneven at times as we traverse the landscape between our cabin and the one behind it. My hands are full carrying the ladder, so I can't carry my own flashlight. The ladder in the yard turned out to be a blessing, though maybe if it wasn't there originally, then Emily wouldn't have tried using it and we wouldn't be in this mess in the first place.

Whatever the case, here we are.

We're trying to be as quiet as possible, whispering whenever we need to communicate, but I'm not sure it even matters. The people who live in the cabin, or maybe just renting it, don't seem to be around. I think if there were people here, and they saw the footage, we would have been thrown into a jail cell a while ago. So while taking precautions is a good idea, I'd rather be as quick as possible. I don't care if I make noise as I walk.

Once we reach the back wall of the cabin, I stand under the red light of the camera. Now I can clearly see it, and it's obvious that Stella was right. It's pointed directly at the backyard of our cabin. By the angle, I think it can peer over the fence, and considering the accident happened as far from the fence as possible, it more than likely caught every single thing that happened.

I prop the ladder up and give it a shake to check that it's stable enough. "Wanna go up, or should I?" I ask Stella.

She looks up and down the ladder, shaking her head. "I don't do well with heights," she says.

The ladder isn't that high, but I don't push the issue. I know if I did, she would give me an earful. Stella has no problem speaking her mind and taking it out on me if the mood strikes her. Besides, climbing a ladder might just be the easiest part of this whole weekend.

Once I'm up there, I feel around the camera. I wish it were as simple as bashing it and being done, but that would only work if it hadn't recorded everything already. That's when I see the wire coming from the back of the camera heading into the wall, and I couldn't be more relieved.

"This is good," I say. "There's a cable that goes inside."

"How is that good?"

"It means it isn't wireless and going to the cloud where the owner can see it on their phone," I explain. "So there's a hard drive inside where we can just wipe everything off of it. Hell, we'll just destroy the whole thing while we're at it."

At this point, I don't really care if whoever owns this place knows it was broken into and their video drive was trashed. The worst thing that'll happen is the police come out and tell them they'll look into it, but since nothing of value was stolen, nothing will come of it. And we'll be doubly sure that there's no video evidence of our sins.

"Great, so now what?" Stella asks.

I climb down from the ladder. "Now we're gonna have to break in," I say, acting confident, when really, I have no idea what I'm doing.

"This place is huge," she remarks. "Do you know where the hard drive is?"

I step back and look at the cabin. It's far bigger than the one we're staying at, maybe three times the size from what I can tell. She's got a point. I have no clue where it might be or how the house is laid out inside. I'd like to believe stealing it will be quick, but realistically, it's going to take some time.

"I don't know," I admit. "But we can figure it out."

"And then still have time to bury the body and fill in the grave?" she asks me, her tone bordering on irritation.

"What do you propose?" I ask impatiently, knowing we won't be finished with everything if we have to do both things in one night.

"We split up," she says.

"And what if these people come home?"

"They aren't," she says. "They haven't been here so far, right?"

I shrug, knowing she's right, but now I'm getting nervous about the idea. She picks up on my nerves. "Hello! Hello?!" She starts to bang on the wall. I quickly shush her and grab her hands. She laughs and holds her hands up in a shrug as we listen.

I want to take off running, afraid that someone is going to come out with a shotgun for stepping on their property. But nobody ever comes out. Nobody shouts at us. Nobody does anything.

We're the only ones here.

"See?" she says, sounding way more confident than I feel. "It's empty."

"Alright, so you go in and find the footage and delete it," I challenge her. If she's so sure it's okay, then she can go.

She shrugs. "Fine by me," she says. "Then you can roll your wife's body into the hole."

Crap. I forgot about that part.

"Oh, not so keen on that, are you?" she says derisively, rubbing it in my face. Stella is far more fearless than I would have given her credit for before starting this weekend getaway with her.

"Alright," I say, realizing there's only one option. "You bury her. I'll break in."

TWENTY-SEVEN

Stella surprises me again this weekend. Not by her attitude or tone, not by her ability to think quickly on her feet and make up a believable story on the fly, but by being resourceful. I was ready to break a window with a rock, but she told me to hold on a moment, then proceeded to walk the perimeter of the property, scanning the ground with her flashlight, looking for something out of the ordinary.

What she found was a small statue of a bird in the front yard. When she picked it up, there was a small compartment underneath it.

And just as both of us had hoped, there was a key tucked inside that small compartment.

Now the real question was, if the key was for the front door, was I going to set off some alarm once I entered the cabin?

The door in front of me is much bigger than the front door at our cabin. It's dark, but I can still make out its deep red color. It looms over me, like I'm an archaeologist about to enter a cave, trying to find treasure through a series of booby traps.

I check over my shoulder to make sure Stella is still there. Her presence is enough to build my confidence, and I slide the key into the door. I turn it to the left and feel the lock disengage. Pulling the key out, I place my hand on the doorknob.

It's now or never, I suppose.

I turn the handle and push inward, gritting my teeth, waiting to hear a beeping alarm, giving me a countdown until it alerts everyone in the area and calls the sheriff's department so they can hurry here and arrest us.

But nothing happens.

There's no noise, only the sound of my beating heart trying to calm itself down now that I know there's nothing to worry about. I turn around to Stella, a big stupid grin on my face, and she smiles back.

"Okay, you good here?" she says.

I would much rather we do this together, but if she's willing to handle burying Emily's body, then I suppose this is the least I can do. "I think so," I say. "Just have your phone on you, just in case." Service is terrible up here, but better safe than sorry.

"Of course," she says. "Be quick, and I'll see how far I can get back there." She points in the direction of our cabin, not specifically saying that she's going to bury a body, but I know what she means.

I step into the cabin, closing the door behind me. I don't know why, but I turn the latch to lock the door, too. Maybe force of habit. Maybe I just don't want anyone to come home randomly and notice their door is unlocked. Though, that's not going to happen, I remind myself.

The living room alone seems the same size as our entire cabin. The ceiling is vaulted high, making it feel much more open. The furniture is large, filling the room appropriately.

It looks more rustic than where we're staying, more like what I figured a cabin would look like up here.

I walk through it, avoiding bumping into the furniture now that my eyes have fully adjusted, scooping up the bits of light they can from the moon, various night lights plugged into the wall, and a glowing clock mounted on the wall. Once I get to the other side, I see where the layout splits into two different hallways. One heads upstairs and to the left, the other veers to the right, still on the first floor. I try to figure out where I am in relation to the back wall where the camera cable disappeared. I spin around, holding my hands out, as if that's going to help me.

It's right then, while I'm deep in concentration, that I hear a sudden clatter.

My heart skips a beat, and I grab my chest, shoving my back against the closest wall I can find. I listen carefully, trying to listen for footsteps or anything else that will give me a sense of the source of the noise.

Nothing happens.

I take a step toward the sound. I'm moving slowly in case someone might be around. Moving toward the sound might not be the best idea, but I need to see it with my own eyes.

I hear an appliance humming the closer I get to where I heard the clatter. I step on the tile of what looks to be the kitchen and see a large refrigerator just on the other side. The humming is coming from there, and I finally realize what caused the clatter.

I pull open the freezer portion of the side-by-side refrigerator and spot the ice maker with freshly made ice in its bin. I snicker softly at my nervousness and stupidity.

"Okay, Joel," I say to myself now that I'm sure I'm alone. "Let's go find this hard drive."

Instead of searching room by room, I go back to where I was before, knowing I'll have time if I can pinpoint the spot where the cord enters the wall. It was on the first floor, I'm sure of it.

I take the hallway leading to the right, knowing it will lead me to the wall the camera is mounted on. I pass a bathroom decked out with a bear-themed shower curtain and towels, but there's no hard drive there. I see a bedroom to my left that is fairly barren, save for a bed and dresser. There's not even a nightstand next to the bed.

I approach a closed door to the right, so I quickly open it and take a peek. The air changes as I stick my head into an empty garage. I never even noticed a garage door outside the house, but Stella and I never walked around this side of the cabin. The people who own this place are much more bougie than the owners of our rental. I pull back into the hallway and close the door again.

I push on until I come to a room at the end and know it must house the hard drive. There's a bookshelf full of books and a desk right in the center. It's the office, and where there's an office, there's usually a computer.

I practically jump over the desk just to get on the other side of it, looking for anything that tells me it would have the footage on it. I pull all the drawers out, look underneath the desk, and even around the sides.

There isn't a computer in here.

I'm ready to pull my hair out. Where the hell is this thing? I plop down on the leather computer chair and spin around, scanning the wall. I know this is the wall where the camera is, so why isn't the hard drive here, too?

That's when I see the small cable coming out of the wall. It looks just like the one going into the wall from the outside. About a foot of cable comes out of the drywall inside, takes a sharp turn to the left, and then disappears, but not into the wall. It vanishes into the ceiling.

That must be where the second story begins. That must mean the hard drive is upstairs.

I spring up from the chair, knowing I've narrowed down its location. I just have to find it on the second story.

But before I can step out into the hallway, I hear a rumble, followed by a creak. I freeze as I notice the wall to my left shaking.

I'm very familiar with that sound and motion. I've experienced it at my own house.

It's not an ice maker clattering a few cubes in the freezer.

No, that's the sound of a garage door sliding up.

Somebody is home.

TWENTY-EIGHT

This is why I wanted Stella to stick around. If she had taken the top floor, then we'd have found the hard drive by now. At the very least, she could have waited outside, giving me a heads-up that the owner was coming back.

Of all times, why did they have to come home now? They weren't here earlier—we haven't seen a single soul up here the entire time we've been here. Except for Deputy McNosy, that is. But this weekend couldn't give us any breaks, could it? We just had to have one more thing go wrong.

What's the worst that could happen? I asked myself before the trip.

Oh, maybe your wife will get crushed by an air conditioner. And you'll break into a house, only to be caught by the owner. Oh, don't forget that you'll take a heavy beating.

Sheesh.

But no time to bitch about it now. I need to get out of here, and fast. But I can't leave this place without wiping the drive first.

I hear the door leading into the garage open, followed

by the garage door sliding back down with a low rumble. The door is right outside this room—I'm gonna have to hide. I spin around, feeling like I'm only going around in circles and making myself dizzy until I find a spot to tuck myself into. There's a space between the bookcase and the wall. If someone enters this room, they won't see me.

But if they spend any longer in here than a quick peek, I'm toast. And there's no time to run out of the room and find a better spot.

I'm just glad I decided not to turn any lights on while making my way around the house.

The door from the garage leading into the house slams shut as I hear a man clear his throat. He lets out a long sigh and flips on the light switch to the hallway. "Oh, what a drive," he says to himself, unaware that he's not alone in the house now. A long, wet-sounding fart follows as confirmation.

If it were any other situation, I might be stifling a laugh right now.

I try to keep my anxiety as low as possible, but at this point, I have no control over it. My heart is racing, and all I can do is pray he goes somewhere else in the house. The worst thing that could happen is that he turns right into the hallway. Then I'll know he's heading for this office.

I listen carefully for what seems like an eternity. I've never stood in my own hallway for this long when I first get home. What is taking him so long? At this point, I just want him to make a decision so I can prepare.

And then I hear him clear his throat again, ever so slightly closer. The man has an allergy problem or some-thing, because the amount of phlegm he seems to be hacking up is a lot. But I'll take it since it's telling me where he's headed.

And right now, he's coming my way.

I brace myself, expecting him to come running around the corner, pointing a finger at me while yelling, "Caught you!" That's dumb, I know, because it's going to be so much worse.

The light flicks on, illuminating the entire room, and I know for sure I'm boned.

He walks in, gliding right past the bookshelf where I hide behind. He's a shorter man, a little wide in the midsection. He has a thinning spot on the back of his head. He looks to be in his sixties from what I can tell.

And in a moment, I'm sure we'll be looking at each other's faces. I don't know if I should run, get into a defensive stance, or maybe even go on the offensive. I'm not looking to hurt the guy, but I'm also not looking to get arrested.

And then he stops in the room, just beyond the desk. He looks down at his feet and fiddles with something. He sure does like to take his sweet time, but this might work to my advantage. He doesn't seem in a rush to turn around, so I take the softest step possible out from the bookcase behind him.

I think all the light thoughts I can—feathers, pillows, clouds. I'm so stealthy that if a mouse farted right now, the man would hear him instead of me.

I shimmy close to the bookcase toward the door, keeping my eyes locked on the man as he crouches down to mess with his shoes or the leg of the desk. I have no idea what he's doing, but I'm so grateful for whatever it is.

I quietly turn around and make it through the doorway. I pick up the pace, tip-toeing down the now-smelly hallway until I make it to the living room.

I can't believe that worked.

I can see the front door across from me through the living room. It would be so easy to just quietly unlock the door and slide outside as if I was never here. If the man spots me then, I could just say I was walking in the area. That would be weird, just taking a walk at night, but not a misdemeanor. Or is breaking and entering a felony?

Who cares? It's a crime. That's all that matters.

But if I leave now, I won't have the video footage. And even if I wasn't arrested now, I would be later. And whatever is on that footage is most definitely a felony, far worse than just breaking and entering. So no, I can't leave until I have deleted that footage.

The idea of waiting until this guy leaves the house to leave crosses my mind, but there's still the chance that he sees the footage in the meantime. And what if he doesn't leave for a few days? I'm sure the place is stocked with everything he needs to hang out here for a while.

It's gotta be now.

I turn to the stairs, knowing it has to be up there. If I'm quiet enough, I'll bet I can find the hard drive and get this done. Then I'll need to figure out how to leave undetected, but I'll worry about that after I've found it.

I take each step as quickly and softly as I can, thinking nothing but light and airy thoughts again. The carpet helps dampen my steps, and I just hope there isn't a creaky floorboard underneath.

Once I'm to the top, the layout seems self-explanatory. Only one way to head now with a few doors lining the wall, leading into various rooms. I move as fast as possible, trying not to pick up my feet but let them glide. I scan each room as I move, evaluating the likelihood of seeing a hard drive.

Bathrooms are a no. A small room with an elliptical machine, some free weights, and a bench is a no. There's a guest bedroom—at least, I think it's for guests, given that it's surrounded by a bunch of scrapbooks and has a table filled with scissors and glue, making me think it's more of a hobby room than a bedroom. I doubt this man is storing video footage in there, but I can always circle back to it.

Then there's the last room, which I can already tell is the master bedroom. An upholstered king-sized bed is smack dab in the middle of the floor. And when I pass through the doorway, I am so happy at what I see.

Along the right wall is a small table where a computer sits. It has a live feed pulled up on the monitor, but the screen shows more than just the one camera. There are a few different images of the perimeter of the house. It's too dark to make anything out in the distance where our rental is, but just like we suspected, the cameras provide a full view of the area.

In the daytime, I'm sure it's far easier to see what's going on, and we spent all day digging back there. Now I just have to figure out how to access the videos I need to delete.

Before I can figure that out, I hear the owner clearing his throat—this time, much closer in the house. He's in the living room, and he isn't as stealthy as me. I can hear every single one of his footsteps as they hit each stair, heading straight up.

And the most likely place he's headed is this bedroom.

Even worse is what I see when I look around for a place to hide. Because the best thing I can see to duck behind is a tall, black, metal gun safe. It tells me everything I need to know about how this homeowner might deal with someone breaking into his house.

I pull my phone out, wanting to text Stella, but there's no service. There's a password-protected WiFi available in this house, but I sure as hell won't be asking for it.

I'm on my own.

I turn to the computer and look underneath the desk. It's not a computer tower like I'd thought, but a DVR specifically for the cameras. It looks like the one I have at work, so I'm familiar enough with it. I grab it and yank all the cords out of it. The screen on top of the table goes black.

I can deal with deleting it later. Right now, taking the whole damn thing is the best plan. And with the footsteps growing closer and closer, I won't be taking this anywhere if I can't figure out how to get out.

In the corner of the room, about four feet from the gun safe, is a window. I rush to it, running around the bed as I do, and peer through the glass. Dark woods surround the home, and as far as I can tell, there's nothing below the window. Not my favorite idea, but a two-story jump isn't the worst thing I've had to do this weekend.

I set the DVR down as I fiddle with the two window latches. They're tough, but I put a little elbow grease into it and get them to pop open.

I hear the man coming down the hallway. I need to move faster.

I put my shoulder into the window, trying to slide it up. At this point, I don't even care if I'm that quiet. If I can make it out before he sees, I can take off running and he'll never know who I am.

The window gives way, and I stumble against the wall, sliding it all the way up. I turn, grab the DVR, and stick a leg out the window, bringing my body out with it so I'm straddling the windowsill, one hand clinging to the DVR, the other to the inside of the room.

I hear the man clear his throat and turn to see the shape of his body entering the room. Holy crap, this is way too close. I don't even have time to think—I just let go with my one hand and close my eyes. I brace for the dropping sensation in my stomach and the ground to come at me fast.

But it doesn't.

I'm tugged back, thinking it's all over. But when I open my eyes, my pants are pinched in the window frame, keeping me from falling out.

The man steps in. He hasn't noticed me sitting in the window yet, but I can certainly see him.

Now I know it's all over.

TWENTY-NINE

A doorbell rings, echoing throughout the whole house. The man spins in the opposite direction from me, not having seen me yet.

"Who the hell is at my door at this hour?" he grumbles.

I'm frozen in the window, not daring to make a single movement to draw his attention away from the door. All it would take is one quick turn of his head and I'm busted.

But he doesn't. Instead, the doorbell rings again, this time sounding in rapid succession. It's annoying and incessant, which is exactly what I need for a distraction. Not looking too happy about it, the man leaves the room.

"I swear this better not be some ding-dong ditch bull-crap," he says, his voice getting further away as he heads downstairs toward the door. "I'm coming, alright!" The doorbell doesn't stop until I hear him disengage the lock and pull open the door.

"Sorry to bother you," I hear Stella say from the front door. Her voice is muffled due to the distance, but it's her sweet, soft tone, and I am so grateful to hear it. "My car broke down on the highway, and I was hoping I could get some help."

I have no idea how long she's going to keep him distracted, but I don't want to try and find out while still in the house. I grab at my pants and work the fabric back and forth until they are no longer pinched in the windowsill. Turning back outside, I swing my leg out and fall to the ground below.

This time, I don't close my eyes but try to plan the landing. The ground comes out of nowhere in the darkness, and I hit a soft spot of pine needles and crumple to the ground, tucking into a roll. My body flares up at every sore muscle from yesterday's beating and the day spent digging. The whole thing feels sloppy, but I make it in one piece, and other than some aches in my heels and knees, I don't think I'm any more injured than I already was before jumping out the window.

I scramble to my feet and walk toward the front of the house. I keep close to the wall, trying not to be caught after all that, but I want to check on Stella. I cling the DVR to my chest as I move.

"You're really lucky," I hear the man say warmly, his entire demeanor changed. I don't know if he's just friendly in general or if Stella has a way about her, but he seems awfully chipper to talk to her despite the late hour. I suspect he'd be far less helpful if the roles were reversed and I was the one asking for help. "I just got in town tonight," he continues. "If you came an hour ago, this place would have been empty."

"Wow, I can't believe my luck," Stella gushes, and I am right there with her on that one. The owner of the house doesn't detect the sarcasm in her voice, but I know the truth.

Our luck on this whole weekend has been downright abysmal. Not even absent, just straight-up bad.

"Come on," he says. I can just barely see Stella at the doorway now. She doesn't notice me, or she's pretending not to because she doesn't look in my direction. Instead, she steps inside, and the owner closes the door behind them.

I'm not sure what Stella's planning on doing or how she's going to get out of this, but she must have seen him come home and came to save my ass. She's so quick to think on her feet that I'm not too concerned about her being inside with this man. I bet she'll get a ride to the gas station, and from there, she can call me. Or, hell, she'll probably get a lift from someone else after giving them some other sob story she makes up on the spot.

I hear the garage door sliding up on the opposite side of the cabin. A car fires up, and I hear the tires crunch over the pine needles in the cabin's driveway, circling around to the front, where the road leads down a hill. The headlights shine across the house for a brief moment, but I stay against the wall to not be seen.

The car idles for a moment while Stella points through the windshield. The interior light flicks on for a moment, and I get a better look at them. The man looks out to where she is pointing, which is away from me and toward the road. Then Stella furtively looks my way and spots me. I lock eyes with her, and she offers me a slight smile. It's almost apologetic, like she's saying sorry for how close I came to getting caught in the house. Or maybe for not coming with me in the first place.

Either way, it doesn't matter because she got me out of it. I lift the hard drive like it's a trophy I just won. She continues to smile, mouths *sorry*, then lifts her hand to her lips, kisses her palm, and blows me a kiss through the window.

Even after everything we've been through, it still feels like there's a connection between us. I don't think she can deny that, either. Only earlier in the day, I was thinking that we'd never want to see each other after this weekend, but there's something about her that I can't shake.

She motions with her eyebrows and chin toward the cabin, telling me to go before they drive off. I watch them leave and head back to the rental. I know she'll get herself back in no time, but right now, I need to get this DVR out of here and find out how much work is left to be done on the burial.

I make my way back to the cabin, this time able to carry my phone and use it as a flashlight since my hands aren't full with a ladder. Stella was able to take it back herself, clearly able to navigate better in the dark than I can.

But the walk is simple enough, and I head straight to the backyard to see what Stella was able to do while I was busy nearly getting caught red-handed inside that person's house. And what I see is a shock.

The entire hole is filled in. The tarp with the body is no longer in sight. A few small piles of dirt are scattered around, but nothing that a hose wouldn't be able to wash away. Was I really gone that long? How was Stella able to get all of this done so quickly?

I'm stunned, but also grateful. The dirt must have been soft and broken up since we dug it up, so Stella could work much faster because of it. She definitely wasted no time, and now I can put my mind at rest, knowing I won't have to be up all night, filling in the grave.

All I have to do is wait for Stella to get back. She can tell me the story she fed to the man—if I even care to know it—

and then we can figure out our stories about this weekend. The hardest part is done. Now we just have to move on.

I head inside, set the DVR on the kitchen counter, then pour myself a drink from the bottle of whiskey I brought for the trip. I haven't even had a chance to enjoy a sip until now, and it tastes like the perfect reward for everything I've had to deal with up to this point.

And I hope deleting the footage is the last thing I have to deal with.

But naturally, nothing can be as simple as that.

THIRTY

It's been about fifteen minutes, and I haven't heard from Stella. Fifteen minutes might not be a lot of time for her plan, but I have no idea what that plan even is. Getting antsy, I decide to go outside and take a look again. Maybe she'll be coming up the way, or maybe there's something I missed about the backyard that I need to clean up. I was so happy that the hole was filled that I just wanted to get a drink and rest.

I get up from the chair in the living room and head to the front door. The DVR is still sitting on the counter, and I eyeball it for a moment. I should just smash the thing right now, but I'm no tech wizard. I want to make sure everything is good and erased before just punting the device against a rock and thinking I'm in the clear.

Sheesh, I can't wait until this paranoia goes away. But for now, I'd rather that than the alternative, which is me getting caught, cuffed, and tried for murder. No amount of "it was an accident, I swear" would do me any good at this point.

Besides, after what happened to Angela, what would

people think? They would dig so deep into my past. Everyone would learn everything I did, everything that happened to her. Keeping all these secrets is the whole reason I'm in this mess now. All because I worry about what people will say, how they'll look at me. And what will become of me after that?

I grab the DVR on the way out, giving in to the paranoia. I decide I don't want this thing out of my sight for even a minute.

It's cold outside now, the temperature dropping far lower than I remember it being the night before. I'm reminded how much I didn't prepare for the weather up here, having figured we would be inside—in the bedroom—almost the whole time. Not outside digging graves.

Even with the relief of being at the tail end of this...journey...it doesn't feel like everything is settled. I suppose it may never feel that way, but I know there are still a few loose ends, like the one in my hands right now. And the question of where Stella is.

I go back to the yard and walk the perimeter. I thought Stella had done a good job before, but now, I really believe it. Even the dirt seems to be pretty level where the grave is. I walk on top of it, patting down the dirt with my feet as I do. It's still soft, but in time, it'll look like nobody has ever disturbed this spot. A little weathering will go a long way.

I get to the fence and peek over, looking back to the cabin where I was not long ago. To my huge relief, the camera light is no longer on, which means nobody plugged the camera back in and I grabbed the right drive.

In the distance, down the road leading up the drive to the large house, headlights flicker through the trees. I feel the need to hide myself, but I know nobody can see me. And if they can, it's not like I'm doing anything I'm not supposed to. I'm just a guy in the backyard of a cabin he's renting. I'll tell them I don't get to see the stars like this where I live. It's believable.

Stella would be way better at making up excuses than me, but luckily, I don't even need to think of one because whoever's driving does not see me. Instead, the car pulls up to the other cabin, heading straight for the garage. I can't see the driver very well, but he looks like the homeowner.

But he's alone. No passenger.

No Stella.

Puzzled, I pull away from the fence and turn back around. If the owner had time to drive her somewhere and back, shouldn't I have heard from her by now? Shouldn't she have reached out to me?

I take my phone out of my pocket and check. No texts, no calls. I pull her number up and try to call her, but there's no service. I let out a sigh, really wishing I had the conveniences of the city right now. I'm too far away from any WiFi, so I need to get back in the cabin to make the call.

I open the gate, ready to head straight for the front door, but I stop in my tracks as soon as I hear a low rumble. It sounds very familiar, like an engine.

But it's not an engine.

My blood runs cold, and my mouth dries up. Hesitantly, I spin around to see myself face to face with a very angry dog. The same big dog from yesterday. The one who nearly attacked me before Stella shooed him off.

He's frothing at the mouth, his teeth are bared, and he's glaring right at me.

THIRTY-ONE

I'm frozen in fear, terrified to make a move, but I know what will happen if I don't. He doesn't look like the type of dog to just get bored and walk away. He looks more like the type to get bored after ripping you to shreds and no longer having something to play with.

If that's the case with this dog, I'd rather not wait for him to get bored.

How did he even get in the yard again? That's when I remember the ladder we put against the hole, along with the various pieces of wood. That makeshift barrier didn't last long since Emily removed it. And then we used the ladder when trying to get to the camera.

How quickly a dead body made us forget about a dog on the loose.

What happened last time? How did Stella get the dog to leave? My eyes wander around, looking for anything I can use to help me out here.

But Stella didn't even need anything, I remember. In fact, I recall her giving me a look that said there was no way she was going to hit this dog or try to distract it somehow. She just commanded it to leave.

If she could do it then, I can surely do it now.

I have to.

I square up, not making any sudden or jerky movements toward the dog, but I try to assert dominance. At least, it feels like I am. For all I know, I look like an idiot, trying to make myself look bigger.

"Hey!" I yell as loud and deep as I can.

The dog continues to growl at me, never letting his eyes stray away.

"Get out of here!" I move my arm hard and fast, pointing behind the dog.

But instead of whimpering or running off, the dog looks angrier than he had been only a second ago. His lips are pulled back so far, I can see the plaque on his teeth. A long string of saliva glistens in the moonlight as it drips to the ground, only breaking about an inch before it hits the dirt.

That's when the growl gets lower, like the dog is ramping up. He lets out a loud bark, his eyes filled with bloodlust. He shifts his weight toward his haunches.

I know exactly where this is headed.

If I wait even a split second longer, the dog will be lunging right at me, gnashing his sharp teeth.

Not waiting for that moment, I spin on my heels and take off running toward the open gate. I hear the dog barking again, its paws padding hard on the dirt as it runs my way.

I make it past the gate and fling the rickety wood as hard as I can so that it latches right before the dog reaches it. I slam against the wood, feeling the weight of the dog smack against the gate, and then hear the metal latch above me.

The dog whimpers for a moment, but he's still up and

going. I can see him through the spaces in the slats. Thankfully, none of them are big enough for him to get through. I slide down the gate, catching my breath.

"That was too damn close," I whisper to myself between breaths. "Where the hell is your owner?"

Nobody seems to be looking for this dog, except for the deputy earlier today. I'm not even sure if the animal has an owner at this point.

I climb to my feet, deciding that the dog can live in the backyard for the time being, and head toward the street. I'm hoping I'll see Stella in the passenger seat of someone's car, and that the headlights will be hitting the street any minute now.

Of course, that doesn't happen.

Instead, I hear the dog barking again behind me, still a ways back. But the barking isn't coming from the backyard, but further to the side.

And then I realize that the hole was still never covered up.

Unlike last time, the dog didn't just run somewhere else. No, he's not happy with how things ended at the gate. And now he's made his way out and found me again.

"You gotta be kidding me," I grumble.

The dog barks at me, daring me to disagree with reality. He's far up the road and not running, but I know he will be in no time.

I look up at the cabin. I could take off running toward it, but the dog is closer to the front door than I am. I'm sure I won't be able to beat him to it. I'm gonna have to figure something else out.

And I'm gonna have to do it right now because the dog charges at me without warning.

THIRTY-TWO

My legs pump as fast as they can, my shoes not gripping well against the gravel road, but I manage to stay upright and move forward. I know I can't keep up this pace forever, and when I give the slightest glance behind me, I see my speed isn't enough to keep the dog away.

Little by little, he is gaining on me, and I'm gonna have to think fast if I want to get away from him for good.

I wish I had run in the direction of my car, but that would have been too easy, right? I had to do this the hardest way possible. But I think I can get to it by circling around. I just need to find a small street or driveway.

And up ahead to my right is exactly what I need.

There's another cabin in that direction, with a narrow gravel driveway leading up to it. It's not as long as the driveway leading to our cabin, but it's enough for me to use it how I need it. I veer off toward it, the dog close behind.

In the cabin, there's not a single light on and no cars in the area. It must be a cabin without a renter, or maybe the owner just uses it on occasion. Whatever the case, I wish someone was there so I could call out for help. Even though I want to draw as little attention to myself as possible, I also don't want to be torn to bits by this dog.

When I spot a fence to the side of the house, I suddenly have a better idea. I run straight for it, hoping my knees are still in good enough shape. I haven't had to jump a fence since I was a kid. Jumping out the cabin window earlier was a lot different than needing to scale a tall fence.

But I pick up my pace, running straight to it. I know if I can just get my hand on top of the wood, I'll be able to hoist myself up and over.

I jump up, my hand grabbing a wooden post between slats for leverage, and I plant my feet against the fence. I pull as hard as I can with my free hand, the other still gripping the DVR to my chest, using the momentum to reach the top of the fence. I practically feel the dog's hot breath on my ankles, my pants hiking up as I pull myself over.

I land hard on the ground on the other side, but I don't care. I am still in one piece, and if that means a bruised tailbone, then so be it. Gasping, I pull air into my lungs as fast as I can, thinking that if I keep this pace up, I'm gonna have a heart attack. I need to get to the gym more often, that's for sure.

One worry at a time, though.

And the next one is coming right up, because as I look at the backyard, I see that there is no end to it. It just continues on, disappearing into the trees and darkness.

I swivel my head to the left and see about thirty feet of fence. And that's where it stops. The fence is only at the front with a bend to it, and it never connects to anything else.

"What the hell is the point of this?" I grumble, pissed at whoever decided to put this half-assed fence here.

Apparently making the same realization, the dog takes off running toward the end of the fence.

Looks like I'm due for that heart attack after all. But I know where to go this time.

I spring to my feet and head in the opposite direction, where the house extends and another open-ended fence sits. I push hard, ignoring any features in the yard or on the back porch. Any distraction at this point will only end poorly for me.

I circle around the fence and then start down the small trail that loops around. I hear the dog somewhere behind me, no doubt trying his best to catch me.

But I'm not gonna let that happen. I can't let it happen. I won't.

I keep telling myself to push harder and harder.

And then I see my car ahead on the road. I'm glad we parked it down here so that it wasn't spotted in front of the cabin. Stella had a good idea with that one. Fewer questions for the deputy to ask while he was stopping by to find this damn dog that is now chasing me.

I really wish the deputy would have found him.

Finally reaching the car, I fish the keys out of my pocket and unlock it. I grab the handle and fling the door open, diving inside. I lean back to the door and grab the inner handle, turning to my left as I do.

The dog's jaws are right there.

I pull the car door shut as hard and fast as I can, just blocking the snapping jaws from biting into my arm. The dog barks and rams himself against the car door, doing his best to get in.

But it's no use. He's out there, and I'm in here, and I'm not interested in changing that arrangement. Not until he's far, far away from me.

I open the glove box and toss the DVR inside for safe-keeping until I can deal with it later. It just barely fits inside, and I'm able to close it with a little extra force to get it to stay latched. The dog continues to bark at my window, but I ignore him, only wanting to drive away without driving over a paw. Even after all this, I'm not a monster. I don't want to hurt an animal.

I turn the key in the ignition, and it starts right up. *That would have just been the cherry on top of this whole thing if it didn't*, I think to myself. I shift it in gear, feeling all the exertion catch up to me. I can't wait to slide into bed after this night.

I'm not sure where exactly I'm going to go, but maybe I'll drive until I hit the highway and see if Stella is walking back. Or maybe I'll even try to drive to the gas station to check that she wasn't dropped off there.

Whatever the case, I need to navigate these roads in the dark right now.

My eyes are heavy, though. My breath is still catching up to its normal rate. I can't really hear the dog anymore, either; I probably lost him a while ago. Maybe he's happy I'm leaving what he sees as his territory.

The road twists and turns, which I vaguely remember from our trips here, but I feel different. Maybe I shouldn't have drank that booze and then run what felt like a fifty-yard dash. I'm sure that didn't do much for my sobriety.

It's hard to keep my eyes on the road. Hell, I can barely even see the road. I'm just so tired right now.

The road fades in and out, and then it's gone. Instead, I see a tree right in front of me.

I watch it happen in slow motion, but there's nothing I can do to stop it. My body is even slower than ever.

I feel the car jerk. I see the tree right in front of me. Before I know it, my face is jammed against the wheel. There's pain, like a dull throb.

But I'm just so tired.

So I close my eyes and sleep.

THIRTY-THREE

My head is throbbing worse than ever. I feel the hint of a hangover, but I know I didn't drink that much. I've been far further down the bottle before with far fewer physical consequences than I feel now.

On top of that, my neck feels totally out of whack. Like I slept all wrong on it so that not only is it stiff, but all the muscles in my body ache. That one has been a constant this weekend, though.

I open my eyes and see that I'm not in bed. Instead, I'm in my car, my face against the steering wheel.

"What the hell?" I ask myself. Staring through the windshield, I see that I'm not on the road but slightly down a hill near it. The car's front bumper is pushed right up against a tree, and I suddenly remember the previous night. Mostly, anyway.

There's the digging, then the breaking into a house, then the dog chase, and the fact that I still don't know where Stella is. I rub my neck as I sit up and look at myself. Nothing seems broken, which is a good start. I don't see any blood, either. I think I'm okay.

I turn to open the door, but then remember the dog. Pulling my hand back from the handle, I glance out the window. There's no sign of any animal near the car. Still, I should probably just start the car and drive it out of here. I go to turn the key, but it's already turned. I turn it off, then try to start it again. Nothing happens.

I check the gauges and see that I'm out of gas. The car has been idling all night, and now there's nothing left in the tank. I slam my hand against the steering wheel. Again, just my luck this whole weekend.

I grumble to myself as I open the door. It's a cold morning, and though I'm still not dressed appropriately, I don't plan on being out here long. I'm gonna have to return to the cabin, get changed, and then Stella and I will have to come up with a plan for how to get the car out of the ditch. I'm hoping that once it's gassed up, I'll be able to drive it out of there just fine.

That is, until I turn around and see the front tire. It's flat, but more than that, the rim looks mangled. It's sitting on a large rock, bending it completely out of shape. That's not going to be cheap, and from what I've seen of this little town, I doubt it's going to be fast, either.

My grumbling hits a new volume as I walk back to the cabin over the winding roads.

I finally make it up the driveway and to the front door. Nothing looks out of the ordinary. The back gate is closed. Stella is nowhere to be seen, but then again, why would she be outside the cabin? I start to wonder why she would have just gone inside without finding me, but I'll save that discussion for when I see her. I could really use a hot shower right now.

I turn the doorknob, but it doesn't move.

"You've got to be kidding me," I say, realizing it is

locked. I search my pockets, but I don't find a key. Was I the one who had it, or did Stella? I can't even remember at this point, but I think she had it, and we just left the door open. That would make the most sense.

So she did go inside and lock up, then. I'm irritated that she just went to bed without me, not wanting to fill me in or find me. Seems odd to me.

I knock on the door and wait. There's no answer, so I knock again.

"Stella!" I say as loud as I can without yelling. "Let me in! I don't have the key."

Still nothing.

Okay, now I'm getting pissed.

I pound hard on the door. "Stella!" I yell this time, pounding harder and harder.

No answer.

I growl my frustration and walk to the windows, tapping on them all as I go by. I check each one, but they're all locked.

I am not amused.

I check my phone, hoping to have some sort of service or WiFi connection, but it's even worse than I thought. The phone is completely dead.

I'm sure no amount of yelling or knocking will work, and none of the downstairs windows are open. Did Stella drink the rest of the bottle I left out and just isn't waking up right now? That would be the only logical explanation. Clearly, she is home. I sure as hell didn't lock the door.

I head to the backyard and see that the ground is nice and level. The only evidence of a trench is the dirt that looks fresh and soft compared to the other spots in the ground. I'm still impressed at how quickly one person was able to handle that.

I turn and smile, seeing exactly what I was hoping to see. The window upstairs, the one that's missing an air conditioner, is open by about a foot. The ladder is against the cabin wall, inviting me to use it.

So I do. It feels a little silly having to climb up a ladder to go through the top window in the bedroom, but I'm left with no other choice. If I hadn't just had the weekend from hell, I would be worrying about someone seeing me. But I know that me climbing into a window will be the least of my worries if someone saw anything that happened this weekend. I can also easily explain it away as locking myself out of the cabin.

I climb through the open window, tumbling over the headboard and onto the mattress. The sheets are a mess, telling me that someone slept in them. But I don't remember making the bed yesterday, either.

What I do know, though, is that Stella isn't up here.

And even more strange, none of my things are on my side of the room. My phone charger isn't on the nightstand, my luggage isn't on my side of the room. I don't even see my dirty clothes from the previous days on the floor anywhere.

"Stella?" I call out to the open air.

There's still no answer, of course. That would be too easy.

I walk past her side of the bed and stop in my tracks. Her stuff isn't there, either. Well, that's not entirely true— her stuff is there, but it isn't how I remember seeing it. Her suitcase is gone, and there are no piles of her stuff on the floor. Instead, it's like she unpacked everything and made herself right at home. Literally.

There's even a picture on the nightstand with someone. I look at it carefully, seeing that it's some other guy.

"What the hell?" I whisper to myself.

I turn to the stairs and head down them, which is when I am even more confused. Where there used to be pictures of random bears and other cabinesque artwork are now pictures of Stella. Why would she have put pictures of herself up? And when the hell would she have had the time to do this, anyway?

There's her with some older people, who I assume are her parents. There's her with a group of girls when she was younger, maybe just out of college. And then another one with that guy from the nightstand. They're sitting in a car together, smiling.

I get to the bottom of the stairs and see more things that make the cabin look less like a rental and more like a home. A jacket is tossed over the couch, shoes are on the floor, a pile of mail is on the coffee table.

I pick up an envelope and study it. Stella's name is on it, followed by an address.

This address.

How can that be?

I am pulled out of my confusion, trying to connect the dots, when I hear what sounds like a whisper. I stand still, trying to make it out, and think it's coming from the bathroom. I head through the kitchen. I still can't make out what the whisper is saying, but I know it's there.

I reach the bathroom and stand in front of the accordion doors that hide the small laundry closet. That's when I hear the stifled whispers more clearly.

I open the doors and see Stella huddled in a corner next to the washing machine.

"Oh my god!" she screams into a cell phone she's holding to her ear. "He found me!"

THIRTY-FOUR

"Stella?" I ask, seeing her crouched down, tears rolling down her face. She's a mess, with her hair in her face and her eyes swollen. She looks frightened beyond belief. "What's going on?"

"Please don't hurt me!" she yells, still holding the phone. She stands up, putting a hand up as if to block me or maybe stop me from getting any closer. "Just leave, okay?"

I stand, blinking at her. I want to grab her and pull her close. She's clearly upset, and at this point, I wonder what happened with her and the owner of that home behind the cabin. I know it's been a wild weekend, but if he did something to her, I will not let that stand.

"What happened to you?" I ask. "Did that man do something? Where did you go? When did you get back here?" The questions just spill out of my mouth, one after the other. There are so many, and she doesn't answer a single one.

I step forward, but she shrinks backward as if I'm going to hit her. "Stay back!" she yells. "I just called the sheriff, and he's on his way. Just go!"

I stare at her for a moment, no longer moving. She called the sheriff?

"Why did you do that?" The last thing we want is any law enforcement around here. At this point, I wonder if Stella is having a mental breakdown from having to bury my wife's body. "We can figure this out if—"

"I don't know you!" she screams.

I can hear someone on the other line now, sounding like they're trying to talk calmly to her. Stella starts pleading with them. "Please, please tell them to hurry."

"Stella," I say, trying to stay as calm as possible. "I don't know what's going on, but clearly, something happened. You know me. It's Joel." I motion to myself, then hold up my hands to show her I mean no harm. "What happened? Why are your pictures all over the walls?"

I'm not sure why that's where I went, but it is. I've asked just about every other question, so why not that one?

"Because this is my house," she says, no longer screaming, just bawling the words out with her tears.

"We rented this cabin," I remind her.

"*We* didn't do anything," she says between sobs. "I don't know who you are. You just broke into my house."

Before I can say anything else, I hear the front door fly open and slam against the wall. I take a quick look over my shoulder and see two men burst in, brandishing guns. One of them is the deputy from yesterday. The other is dressed in the same uniform.

"Help me!" Stella screams.

"Sir, get your hands up!" the deputy from yesterday shouts at me.

"Look, this is all a misunderstanding," I say evenly. I turn back to Stella to get her to help me out. To tell them we know each other, and that I'm supposed to be here.

"Sir, I said—"

"Look, if you'll just let me—"

"He won't leave me alone!" Stella screams again.

I hear the snap of a trigger and feel a bite on my back and leg. It's not a bullet that has hit me, but two prongs from a taser. The jolt surges through my body.

I hit the ground, jerking uncontrollably. As I writhe on the floor, Stella jumps over me and rushes to the two officers.

THIRTY-FIVE

I try to reflect on everything that has led to this point. Here I am, sitting in the back of the deputy's vehicle, cuffed and waiting to be taken to the station so that I can be put in a cell for who knows how long. I mean, this situation was always in the realm of possibility after deciding to cover up my wife's accidental death, but Stella losing her mind was never at the top of the list for the reasons I'd be here now.

I'm curious how she's going to explain her way out of this one when they ask to see verification that she lives here. Because, at best, she'll have a receipt for renting it out for the weekend. Maybe I'm not on that receipt, but it'll prove she was lying about owning the place. I know whoever was on the other line heard her say that.

That should be able to help me. At least, I sure hope it will.

The deputy comes up to me. The back window is open, and he leans against the car as he talks to me. "So you say you know this lady?" he asks me, his tone suspicious. The way he looks at me is also full of mistrust.

It's going to be an uphill battle out of this one.

"Yes," I say. "We are renting this place for a weekend trip away."

"Weekend trip away? Like as a couple?"

I nod. "That's correct. We have been dating for about a month."

The deputy looks me up and down, which is funny considering that I'm sitting in the back of his car and he's looking through the small window. At first, I think he's trying to imply that I'm too old for her or that she's out of my league. Both of those things are probably true, which is why I was so ecstatic about this weekend, but I finally hear what he's really thinking.

His eyes settle on my hands cuffed in my lap. "Is that a wedding band tan?"

I look down at my finger and see the pale circle around my finger. The one with the same outline as my absent wedding band. I had taken it off for the weekend and never put it back on. I was worried that Stella would have seen the damning circle when we first started seeing each other, but she never commented on it, so I thought it was all in my head.

Clearly, that wasn't the case. But somehow, Stella never noticed it before. Or she never seemed to care about it.

No use in lying to the deputy right now. It's not like he knows Emily is buried on the other side of that fence. "Yes," I admit.

He turns and motions toward Stella, who is speaking to the other deputy. "And she isn't—"

"No," I cut in. "She's not my wife."

"Huh," he says, narrowing his eyes at me.

"Look, I know what you're thinking, and that's fine. My wife and I have been having issues, and maybe this wasn't the best way to deal with them, but—"

"You mean breaking into a house you don't own and claiming you're dating the homeowner?"

I stare at the deputy in disbelief. He's not even listening to me. "That's not fair."

"Fine. Go ahead, tell me."

"I got locked out of the house and chased by this dog," I say. "You were here the other day looking for him, weren't you?"

He nods slowly. "I guess so."

"How would I know that if I wasn't here with Stella?"

"I didn't see you here," he says. "The only person here was the young lady."

"I was in the house," I insist. "I just didn't come out." I'm not going to tell him *why* I didn't come out, but this should be good enough, right?

He shakes his head. "Not according to the lady," he says. "Not unless you were in the area, trying to get close."

I roll my eyes. "I'm not a stalker."

"If you say so."

"All my things should be inside the house!" I yell in frustration. "My suitcase and everything!"

"What about your car?" he says. "That's the one that blew a tire off the side of the road, correct?"

"Yes, that's mine," I say. "We came up together in it."

"Well, we checked the back and saw your suitcase in it," he says. "All your things are inside, and nobody else's."

I don't even know what to say to that. I open my mouth, but the words don't come. I never put my stuff back in the car.

I'm so confused. What is even happening?

"From what it looks like to me, you broke into this woman's house and got caught, so you came up with some strange story to tell us. I'm not really sure what you thought that would accomplish, to be honest."

"What about the reservation?" I point out. "Stella made a reservation to rent this place, so she clearly can't own it, right? She's lying about that."

The deputy takes a deep breath. I can tell he's pretty fed up with me right now. But I know I'm right—he just has to check.

"That's the thing," he says. "We checked her identification. On her license, her address is listed as this very place right here. So if you have proof otherwise, like this supposed reservation, I'd love to see it."

I can't believe what I'm hearing right now. "I, uh, well, she's the one that made the reservation." I feel so defeated right now, like whatever is happening is finally settling in. I'm screwed here, aren't I? And now, I just look crazy. "I didn't have any part in that."

"Doesn't look great," the deputy comments, and his tone is not accusing or even mean. It's matter-of-fact, and I know he's right.

I think if I can just talk to Stella. I can get her to clear this up. I lean close to the window, trying to get a glimpse of her around the deputy. "Stella!" I shout.

She turns to look at me. I see a little bit of sympathy in her face, so maybe there's something there.

"Stella, please tell them. Tell them we came here together. You know we did!"

Her mouth drops open, and she cocks her head, staring at me.

"That's enough, sir," the deputy warns, stepping in front of me.

"Wait," Stella says, sparking hope in me. I don't know

what happened to her, but maybe she can remember now. "I do know him."

"Thank god," escapes from my mouth. The deputy steps aside, and Stella walks toward me.

I look at her face, and she purses her lips as her eyes narrow at me. "Oh my god. It is you, isn't it?" she asks in disbelief.

It is me, but what is she talking about? How could she forget me so quickly? I feel like I'm being majorly gaslit right now, made to feel like a crazy person when she's the one who has clearly lost it. "You're the guy from my doctor's appointment."

"Doctor's appointment?" I repeat blankly.

"I had trouble with my iPad, and you helped me," she says. "Yeah, that's it." She turns to the deputies. "I saw this guy at the medical office building, and he walked me through it. But then he wouldn't leave me alone. Asked to get lunch, but I turned him down. I swear to god, this guy has been bothering me ever since."

"Stella, what are you talking about?" I ask in alarm.

"Stay away from me, you creep," she snaps at me. "I told you no, so leave me alone." Stella turns away and storms off, the other deputy following her.

"Stella!" I shout. "Stella, wait!"

But she goes inside. I turn to the deputy, the one with the name tag "D. Larson," and shake my head. "That's not true. I went to lunch with her. She asked me to go." I am blabbering incomplete thoughts as they run through my head.

"So you did or did not help her with an iPad?" the deputy asks.

"Yeah, but I...it was different," I say, leaning back in the seat. My shoulders slump, and I stare at the deputy, hoping he will have an answer because I sure as hell don't.

All he offers me is a sympathetic smile, like he's acknowledging the anguish on my face.

"I don't understand what's happening," I finally admit.

THIRTY-SIX

They've been asking me questions in a completely white room for what feels like an eternity. I might have been here for only thirty minutes—hell, maybe even ten minutes, for all I know. But it feels far longer than that. Maybe I've been here all day, with them coming in and out, leaving me alone with my thoughts between all their pestering questions.

All I can think about is the interaction with Stella this morning. From her frightened look in the cabin to her claiming she doesn't know me. Or rather, that she only met me the one time and I've been—*stalking* her? Maybe she didn't say "stalking," but she did call me a creep. That I remember.

A single cup of coffee sits in front of me, steam rising from the top. When asked, I told them I take it black, but really, I just didn't care. I pick it up and sip on it, the warmth running down my throat and into my stomach as I fight the bitter taste. Usually, I take cream. A little part of me regrets not requesting it, but the other part is glad I'm drinking it this way. The bitterness is a bit like pinching myself during a dream, reminding me that this is really happening.

By the look on Deputy Larson's face, I think he feels bad for me. Not because he believes me, but he believes that I believe it. Which I do, because it really happened.

God, now I even think I sound crazy.

"I'm telling you, I'm not sure what happened to her, but she is lying or confused or...I don't even know!" I say, my voice raising. I take a deep breath, trying to keep it together. The moment I fly off the handle, I'm sure I'll get locked up, and the cops won't entertain a conversation with me anymore. "Look, she went off with the neighbor and didn't come back right away. Maybe he did something. I don't know."

Deputy Larson sighs. "And this neighbor, you think he'll vouch for you?"

I shake my head slowly. "No, I don't think he saw me."

"Here's the problem," Deputy Larson says. "If the neighbor says he gave Stella a ride but doesn't know who you are, it still doesn't help you. In fact, it makes her story even more credible."

"What story is that?" I dare to ask.

He purses his lips, clearly growing impatient with me. "That you are following her," he says, his accusation clear as day. "But if you have nothing else that will help your case, this is it. I'm gonna have to put you in a cell, and then they'll take you to county for holding."

Is this really happening right now? My confusion is fading away, replaced with anger.

After everything Stella and I went through this weekend, I'm ready to light it all on fire. Not only that, but she clearly didn't expect me to throw myself under the bus, so she never mentioned what happened in the backyard. If I spill the beans first, then I'll have the upper hand. She's already said she doesn't know me, so maybe I'll come out of this fairly unharmed. What I say to the police doesn't have to make complete sense. Just enough that she feels the pressure.

She's going to be totally screwed.

"Look," I say. "I know it looks odd, me saying all this. And that Stella says she doesn't know me. But something happened, okay? She is hiding something from you."

"And what might that be?" Deputy Larson asks.

"About what's in the backyard," I say, swallowing hard right after. My heart races in my chest, and I wonder if this is the right move. But so far, nothing else has worked, and they're talking about sending me to county. And then what? Some sort of trial? I have no clue—I've never been in this position before. But it feels like it's too late. I've already started down this path, so I might as well see it through to the end.

"There was an accident," I say.

"We know," he says. "We towed your car already. It'll be able to be picked up by your spouse or someone else if you'd like."

My spouse, I think. How I wish Emily could pick it up.

"That's the thing," I say. "It wasn't my car. It was my wife. She got hurt. Real bad."

The deputy leans in, now looking much more interested in what I have to say. "You hurt her?"

I shake my head. "No, not me. Stella did." It's not a lie, either. She was the one who pushed the air conditioner out of the window. "I know she didn't mean to do it, but she also didn't want to call you guys. So she buried the body."

"Your wife?" the deputy asks me, his voice full of disbelief. But I think I'm finally getting somewhere.

I nod grimly. I know what I'm admitting to here, but I think I've got the deputy on my side now. "It's crazy, I know, but when she said she was digging up the septic system, she was really digging a grave."

He leans back. "And that's Emily? Emily Rosenthal, correct?" he asks, looking down at a small piece of paper.

I nod. "That's her," I say, feeling it all set in. I'm sure I'll have more explaining to do, but it is such a relief to admit it out loud. Even if I am selling Stella out.

"And this happened—"

"Two days ago," I finish.

A knock comes, and Deputy Larson stands up. "Then can you explain this to me?" he asks.

I frown. "I'll do my best," I say, not sure what he's referring to.

He opens the door, still looking at me. "If your wife is dead, how is she standing right here?" he asks, stepping out of the way.

My breathing stops as I'm confronted with something I have zero explanation for. My mouth is dry, and my brain implodes as I freeze up.

My wife, Emily, who is supposed to be six feet in the ground, stands in the doorway.

"Joel?" she asks. "What is going on?"

THIRTY-SEVEN

Emily

"Thank you for coming so quickly," Deputy Winslow says, even though it was at least a few hours between his phone call and my arrival at the station. He's much older than his partner, Deputy Larson, who was in the room with my husband when I got here. Now they both stand with me, leaving my husband locked in the room behind us.

"Of course," I say. "I just don't understand what is going on. You say he was following some girl? That he was with her on, what, a getaway weekend?"

"That's correct," Deputy Winslow says.

Deputy Larson clears his throat. "He, uh, he also said you were in an accident. That this girl, the homeowner, buried you in the backyard."

He looks at his feet almost apologetically. I can't tell if he's doing it because he's shy and doesn't want to say that I was dead—which, clearly, me standing here says otherwise

—or if he feels sorry that my husband is telling some wild stories that make no sense.

At this point, I can't tell if they think he's lying on purpose or if they think he's lost his mind. I've barely exchanged more than a handful of words with Joel since I got here, so it's too soon for me to make that decision and let them know. But I know I'll be able to soon enough.

I sigh, knowing they don't want to let Joel go, but if I play the one card I have, I think I can get him out of here. "I'm a psychiatrist," I say. It's not a lie. I have no reason to lie for my husband right now, especially after his cover story was that he was cheating on me. "He's been having some hard times at home. It's something I've noticed, and I've tried working on it with him. I just didn't realize that it would progress to, well, this." I motion to the door behind us, and then to the hallway of the station.

The two deputies exchange glances. "We don't appreciate being lied to by him, but if you're saying you can take him, then we'd be okay with that," Deputy Wilson says.

"Of course," I say. "Is there some sort of bail or something that I—"

He shakes his head. "Nothing like that," he says. "The homeowner called us up not long ago and said she felt bad for your husband. That the look on his face told her he had no idea what was happening, and she hopes he can get some help. Said that him ending up in jail wouldn't do anything for his mental health and that she doesn't want to press charges."

My eyes widen. "Oh my god," I say. "That is so great of her."

"But he has been trespassed, so if he is caught on the property, we will arrest him and charge him," Deputy

Winslow says, lifting his eyebrows as he looks at me, as if he was peering over glasses.

"I completely understand," I say. "It's pretty late, so we'll be at the Best Western if you need us. I'll make sure he doesn't bother the woman again."

"And his car is in impound right now," Deputy Larson says. "It's not really drivable, so you'll need to have someone get it and fix it up. I can give you a list of auto shops nearby if you need."

"Thank you," I say. "I'll arrange for all that sometime down the road. I hope it's alright if it isn't first thing in the morning."

He shakes his head. "No rush, just making sure you know."

"Thank you," I say. "And I'll make sure I get him home first thing in the morning. And then we will have a real talk about what's going on."

"That's probably wise," Deputy Winslow says.

THIRTY-EIGHT

Joel

Emily seems a lot calmer than I would have thought. After everything, I figured she would be livid.

But what the hell am I even talking about? I thought she was *dead!*

But here she sits, right in front of me.

The motel is basic but clean, but not exactly a hot spot in town. When we pulled up to it, it looked like a ghost town with only one car in the parking lot. And I am willing to bet money that it belonged to the front desk clerk, who was working the lobby when we walked in.

By the time we left the sheriff's station, it was dark out. I hadn't realized I was in there for so long. It certainly felt like a long time, but I thought that was just because I was stressed out.

Emily had made the trip up from the valley, about three hours from this town, so they must not have called her until later in the day to come get me. According to them, Stella wasn't pressing charges.

As if she had any right to.

But then again, Emily is alive. She's literally living proof of that. And I have nothing but a bunch of words that don't match up with reality.

Emily sits across from me on the second queen bed in our motel room. I'm sitting on the one closest to the door. She brought a bag of things and laid them all out when we first got here. I can't remember all the things that happened once we checked in. I was still in shock. I still am, technically. But after a while, I remember that she told me to sit down so we could talk.

I think that was five minutes ago. We've just been staring at each other while I try to form a coherent sentence to start telling her what happened. But I don't know how. I'm not sure I understand what is happening right now.

I just start talking, letting out whatever comes into my head. It's fragmented and probably the worst way to tell her, but at this point, I'm scrambling to make sense. To just have someone listen to me.

"I thought I was having an affair," I say. And really, wasn't I? I don't even care anymore about sounding like a scumbag. I just want to be sane. "But from what they're saying, I wasn't?" It's a question, and that's exactly how I mean it. Emily is a psychiatrist, so she should be used to this sort of thing. Even if not from me, her husband.

She nods, contemplating my words. "Keep going," she says, slipping into doctor mode, which is probably better than wife mode right now. I need help, not anger or disappointment.

I don't know what to say, though. I *thought* I was having

an affair, but that's not really it. I mean, I really *was* having an affair.

Wasn't I?

"How else would I have known Stella?" I asked aloud. "I know I spotted her, stopped and talked to her, and then we had lunch. But she says we didn't."

Emily stays calm. A man admitting to his wife that he was cheating on her seems like a big pill to swallow, even if he's been only imagining it.

"I know you have been having issues lately," Emily says. "Maybe I wasn't always the best wife to you, but overall, I thought we had a decent marriage. Didn't you?"

I hadn't even stopped to think about that, to be honest. It was all about the young girl who got me excited. I'd felt that spark slip away with Emily, and maybe I wasn't fair to her. To just tell her how I felt—I've never been great at that. Being married to a psychiatrist feels like she always has the upper hand when discussing anything. Maybe this was my way of controlling things.

I think Emily's started to rub off on me after all these years.

"I do," I say. "I'm sorry." I know it's not much, but it feels like I should say it, anyway.

Emily pauses for a moment. "Is there anything else? Something that you're not telling me? Something that maybe led to this?" she asks, her Ph.D. showing hard right now as she pokes and prods until she gets under the scab to discover what I'm really hiding.

And the thing is, I'm still hiding something. I hardly even let myself think about it.

Angela.

"I don't know," I say, shaking my head. The truth is, I really don't know. Is Angela eating at me? Is that why I created this whole scenario in my head? Maybe if I just own up to her, then this will all go away.

That poor girl, but it wasn't my fault. That's what I tell myself, anyway. One thing I do know for sure, though, is that she deserved better.

And then I did it all again with Stella. Was it always going to end up the same way?

Oh, god, what am I even doing right now? The relationship with Stella wasn't even real!

I pull at my hair because that's what my thoughts are making me do. The burn of my scalp brings me back to the present instead of being lost in all those terrible memories, real and fake.

"I'm okay," I say finally. "It's nothing. I think I am having problems. Stress from work, maybe."

Emily takes a deep breath and lets out a long sigh. She's almost in wife mode again, her patience growing thin. That's fine with me. I don't want to talk about it anymore right now, and I really don't want to talk about it with her.

"I think we both need some rest, and we can revisit this tomorrow," she says.

And that's the one thing I can agree with. Though, I know there won't be any rest to be had. Not when my raging mind keeps pulling me back.

THIRTY-NINE

Emily fell asleep hours ago. I didn't get a look at the clock when she did, but it had to be somewhere around ten. Her breathing is steady, and I've been staring at the back of her head, making sure she doesn't stir.

But I know she doesn't. She's not the restless type at night. Once her head hits the pillow, she's out for the rest of the night. A blessing for her, and definitely for me right now.

I am wide awake. I never even went to sleep. But then again, I know in my heart that I never really intended to.

Before lying down, I couldn't shake the idea that I'm right. That maybe this insanity I'm feeling is all fake. That maybe I am insane right now, but in a different way. That the woman in the other bed isn't even Emily.

I saw Emily on the ground. She wasn't moving. She was dead. How could my mind have just snapped and imagined that whole thing?

Of course, I know now that I truly do sound crazy.

But I know I'm not because of one thing.

I hold my hand up to the glowing numbers of the clock

on the nightstand next to my head. There's a small callous on my palm. I scratch at it with my finger, feeling the rough, raw spot.

That callous is fresh. That's not something my mind can just make up.

I was digging a hole in that backyard, wasn't I?

And because of that, there was only one thing on my mind.

I somehow need to confront Stella when there's nobody else around. I need to get her to tell me what really happened and why my wife is still alive, sleeping in the bed next to mine.

I may not know what is happening to me right now, but I'm sure as hell getting some answers from someone who does.

I check on Emily one last time before putting my clothes on. She's still sound asleep. I gently pick up her keys from the dresser and slide out of the hotel room, locking the door behind me.

The drive is easy from here, as I know the way. Another thing that my mind either created or I have real memories of it. It goes by so fast, and now I'm sitting in the driveway, staring at the dark cabin.

It's time to get to the bottom of this.

FORTY

Emily

The slight jingle of the keys scrapes against the dresser, and I know what Joel is planning. I hear the lock on the door slide open before Joel quietly sneaks out, closing the door ever so gently. But I can still hear it all.

Then again, I was just pretending to sleep.

I hop out of bed and check the bathroom to make sure he isn't hiding in there. It's empty, so I know I'm right about what he's doing. The missing keys confirm my hunch.

I check the clock, timing it to when he left.

"Joel?" I call out to the emptiness.

There's no answer.

I flip the light on and plop back down on the bed, leaning against the headboard. It's been a rough weekend for him. At least, from what I understand.

He's still hiding that secret from me, and I wish he would just open up about it completely. Instead, he is clutching it harder than ever. The remaining thing he doesn't want to reveal to me.

Joel and his stupid secrets.

They're going to get him in a lot of trouble. I've always known it, for our entire marriage.

But he would never listen to me.

I tried warning him that it wouldn't end well, and now I'm afraid he's going to find out firsthand.

I slide my clothes on, but I'm not in a rush. I don't have a car right now, what with Joel driving it and all. Besides, he needs some time to work through things, right?

I will admit that he hasn't seemed himself lately, as I told the deputies and Joel himself. It's like something inside him is broken.

I really wish he could have come out and told me what was really on his mind. Those damn secrets of his. If he did, I could have helped fix everything. But Joel has to be stubborn. Has to do everything himself.

So, I'm going to let him. I'm going to sit here and give him that time.

And once I think it's been long enough, I'll call the police.

FORTY-ONE

Joel

I've been pounding on Stella's door—or is it the rental's door?—for at least five minutes straight. She doesn't answer. No matter how many times I tell her through the door I just want to talk.

She's not there. Or maybe she's hiding like last time, calling the police again.

But this time, I'm not going to let that happen.

I do the same routine. I climb up the ladder and into the window. It's dark inside, and there are no signs that she's around. The bed is completely made up this time, like she never even tried to sleep in it.

"Stella!" I yell out.

But of course, there's no answer.

Instead of wandering around, I head straight for the laundry closet, passing all the pictures of Stella in various moments of her life. I'm still baffled how she managed that one, but she will tell me once I find her.

I'm going to make her tell me.

I slide open the accordion doors, expecting to see her in the same position as earlier in the morning. Technically, it's the next morning now, but since I never went to sleep, I think it still counts as the same day.

But she's not there. She's not huddled in the corner on her phone. Hell, she's not even waiting for me with a baseball bat or some other weapon.

I run through the cabin, turning over every little thing I think she could hide around, under, or inside. The place isn't big, so it doesn't take me long.

She's nowhere to be found.

Did she leave? Really? After all that, and she bailed on me?

That's fine, because I don't need her to prove what we did. I know exactly where to find it and how to get to it.

I walk outside, open the gate, and step into the backyard. There's no light, but that doesn't matter. I can see just fine with the moonlight. I know the exact spot I need to be digging, anyway.

I pick up a single shovel from the side of the cabin and stand in front of the spot where the soil has recently been disturbed.

If my wife is in the motel room, then who did we bury here? I can't be hallucinating Emily being alive, because then the deputies wouldn't have seen her. Besides, whose car did I drive to get here? Mine is locked up right now, unable to be driven because of the busted rim.

So that means this weekend had to have happened, though I'm still flipping back and forth on which level of insane I am right now.

But why did Stella lie?

Maybe there's something even worse here. Maybe it wasn't my wife we killed, but someone who looked a lot like her.

The whole thing seems preposterous, but I'm at my wit's end. I plunge my shovel into the dirt, deciding that I have to see for myself who is buried in this grave.

FORTY-TWO

Emily

The room is awfully quiet as I think about what Joel is up to. I decided to give him a lot more time than I figured I would. *Can't be too careful*, I thought. I've been ready for hours, saw the sun come up through the window, and watched the traffic pick up as the morning light streamed in.

I think it's been enough time in this lonely room, and now I should think about heading out to find Joel.

Even after all that's happened, a little part of me hoped it wouldn't have come to this. That Joel would have just opened up, told me his secrets, and stayed in the damn room all night so we could be a family again. His sins could have been forgiven. But no, he had to double down.

I feel bad for him. He's still my husband, even with everything he's done to me. To Stella.

And to Angela.

I smile to myself, though I'm not amused at all. He

might believe I never knew about her, but I did. Once again, another slip-up from Joel. That pesky rewards number and him being too cheap to pass up the chance to get points. He never learned then, and he may never learn now.

He's a creature of habit. So very predictable at this point.

In my line of work, it almost becomes a game.

But I never did confront him about it. Was that wrong of me? I don't think so. I was trying to give him the time to own up to it.

And I never got angry at Angela, either. I saw her for what she was—a young girl desperate to have someone, just like the rest of us. Someone who not only told her all the right things, but followed through on them. Little did she know that Joel was never going to be that person for her. The poor thing fell too hard for someone who could never deliver. Someone who made nothing but a bunch of empty promises.

I know this. I've been married to him for twenty years.

And I know that when he is done with someone, there is no mistaking it. He. Is. Done.

Ending things comes easily to him, maybe because I'm here. He always has me to fall back on to keep him normal. Keep him grounded. Keep him sane.

But somewhere along the way, I faded to the background of his life. Unappreciated, taken for granted, and brushed off like I don't have feelings of my own that deserve consideration.

I know Joel has good in him. He's not an evil man. He's honestly not even all that bad. Just made a series of bad decisions that have turned into a hole he can't dig himself out of.

And Angela was one of those decisions.

He never meant to hurt her. I know that. And physically, he didn't. But she had attachment issues. That was clear as day, and I never even met the girl. But I remember the phone calls late at night, the random notes left around the house, and Joel's struggle to cover everything up. To make her go away.

And then, she did.

But not in the way he intended.

Reading a brief article about a girl who was so depressed and lonely that she swallowed a bunch of pills so she would never wake up was horrible. But that happens every day. Doesn't make reading about it any easier, but it feels so far away when it isn't someone you know.

But when an email from this girl shows up in your inbox, highlighting all the reasons she felt wronged, all the reasons she wished she was me so she could be with Joel, and why she was ending her own life...well, then it gets a little more personal.

I'm sure we could have gotten along in another life. I'm sure you're a nice person. But I don't understand how he can keep going back to you when he has me. He came to me for a reason, and now he's going back to you. I hope you can make him happy. I didn't.

Her words written on the screen pierced a hole right through my heart.

Because clearly, it didn't matter to Joel that he was with me. It didn't matter to him that he had abandoned Angela.

Here we are now, repeating history in some ways. But this time, Joel isn't himself anymore.

FORTY-THREE

Joel

I've been at this all night, or at least from when I got here in the middle of the night until now, and I still haven't reached the bottom. But by now, I feel like I should have. The sun is up now, and I'm more confused than ever. How did Stella fill in this hole all on her own? Maybe filling it in is different than digging it up, but still, she didn't have all this time like I've had.

Either way, I still have more to go.

My muscles are screaming at me, my palms blistering underneath the garden gloves, and I'm drenched in sweat despite the chilly breeze. I am exhausted, and I can't wait to be finished. Not just so I can rest, but so I can finally have answers.

The pile of dirt is high, blocking my view of the gate as I stand in the grave about six feet. I'm so close, I can feel it. I just need to push on a little longer, a little further, then I can finally take a break. That's what I've been telling myself for a while.

But part of me is worried. When I get to the bottom of the hole, what if there is no bottom? That all there'll be is a big, empty hole in the ground. Maybe a septic line.

If my wife isn't buried here, that should be a relief, right? But what will that say about me? About my mental state? Have I really lost it? Gone insane? I don't feel insane, but then again, isn't that the whole point? If I knew I was insane, then I truly wasn't.

Were those memories all fake?

I dig my shovel into the dirt one more time, lifting a huge scoop and tossing it. The scent of the earth was fresh when I started, but my nose can't smell it now. Accepting that this is what I'm used to, like I'm going to be here forever.

My clothes are stained brown, but I don't care. The exposed skin on my arms is caked in dirt, creating a barrier against any elements I come across. I feel like I'm not only going to be here forever, but that I'm part of this earth now. That where I begin, the earth ends, and vice versa.

Maybe I am going insane?

Before I can answer myself, I hear the gate creak open, and footsteps enter the yard. I'm no longer alone back here.

I spin around, ready to find Stella and demand answers. I start to climb out of the hole, still unable to make out who it is around the pile of dirt, but when I get halfway up, I am met with a gun pointed right at me.

"Stay put!" Deputy Larson yells at me.

I freeze, teetering on the edge of the hole, unsure if I should put my hands up and fall backward or keep my hands planted in the dirt to stay propped up.

"Do you have any weapons on you?" he asks.

"No, sir," I say.

He motions behind him, and Deputy Winslow steps into view. He looks far more irritated than Deputy Larson, like I'm ruining his day by forcing him to be up and at it already. Deputy Larson holsters his gun and pulls me out of the hole.

When he's done, he rolls me over and cuffs me. "We told you that you were trespassing here," Deputy Larson says. "Now we have to charge you with trespassing. You know that, right?"

I sigh. "I was just trying to get answers," I say. "I swear, Stella and I were here together. I just want to know why she's lying about everything."

"You can't be here," Deputy Winslow growls.

"So, what, you just dug up her yard?" Deputy Larson asks.

"She wasn't here for me to ask questions," I say. "So, yes, I dug up her yard. How did she even know I was here to call you?"

I watch as they exchange glances. "She didn't call us," Deputy Larson says. "It was your wife. Said you left the hotel and seemed erratic."

I guess I can't blame Emily for that one. It's not like I gave her much to go on, and then I just left her at the hotel without her car. "I'm telling you, I'm so close, I can feel it," I say. "Please, let me dig until I get to the bottom."

I watch them shake their heads, and Deputy Larson pulls me to the gate. "Just give it up," he says. "It's time to go."

I'm so done with this. I'm sure I've seemed crazy enough, but I'm just going to let it out again. "Stella killed my wife, okay?! I know this. Her body is buried right here!" I'm screaming now. I know it doesn't make any sense, but I have nothing else to lose. I mean, maybe I have a lot to lose, but I don't care anymore.

I can see from the looks on their faces that they think I'm nuts. They seem to even pity me. But I don't want their pity. I want them to believe me.

"Joel," Deputy Larson says, his tone softer and compassionate. "Your wife called us. She picked you up at the station, remember? She's alive."

I have no argument for that because I saw her with my own eyes, but I just can't take it anymore. I feel the sobs bubble up in my chest, and tears run down my face. "I know," I admit. "I just don't understand."

I hear a scratching in the hole behind me, and so do the deputies. We all take a look, but I can't see anything from my vantage point. Deputy Winslow goes to check it out.

"There's a dog down here," he says. "Hey! Get out of there, go!" He waves his hands, and the dog climbs out of the hole, making the action look far easier than when I came out. It's the same dog I encountered when I first arrived here with Stella. The one that chased me to my car.

"Careful," I say. "He's not very friendly."

The dog stops and looks at me, cocking his head to the side, trying to study me. Deputy Winslow approaches him and pets him on the head. The dog looks like he's smiling, his tongue hanging out of his mouth. "Seems pretty friendly to me," he remarks.

I sigh. Just another cherry on top of this weekend. Is everyone, the dog included, here to gaslight me?

Deputy Larson turns me back toward his vehicle, but Deputy Winslow stops us. "Hold up," he says. "We got something here."

We turn around again, and Deputy Larson walks me to the hole. "What is it?" he asks.

"It's a body," Deputy Winslow says.

"I told you I wasn't crazy!" I say, far more excited than I should be. But I feel vindicated right now that I wasn't going crazy. That maybe they will listen to me now.

Deputy Winslow gets in and brushes some dirt to the side. When he does, we can all see a motionless face emerge from the ground. There's no tarp covering her up. And it is a her.

A car drives up from the street. The door slams shut, and the car drives off. I take a quick look to see Emily running up to the gate and through it to the backyard, joining us.

"Ma'am, you need to stay back!" Deputy Larson calls out, but does nothing to physically stop her since he is still holding me.

Emily looks deeply concerned. "What are you doing here, Joel?"

But I don't answer her. I have no words right now. Instead, I watch as Deputy Winslow uncovers more of the woman's face, and immediately I know who it is.

It's not my wife. Which makes sense, considering she is standing right next to us.

It's Stella.

"Stella?" I gasp. "I don't—"

"Oh my god," Emily says, her voice trembling. "That's Stella Brisbane. She's my patient!"

FORTY-FOUR

Emily

"You didn't tell me the name of the woman whose house Joel broke into," I say to the deputies.

The two deputies watch me as if I hadn't revealed any information to them, when really, it was their own lack of information that kept me from giving them anything that might have been important.

"We didn't think it was pertinent information at the time," Deputy Winslow says, shifting in his chair.

"That's fair," I say. "So I wouldn't have thought to just reel off every patient I've ever had. That's almost like asking me to reveal every person I've ever met. If you wanted to know if I knew the woman, you should have told me who she was in the first place." I cross my arms, talking down to them.

I'll be damned if I just sit here and take their disapproving looks when it was their own lack of foresight that led to their mishandling of things.

I watch as they soften their expressions. They know I'm right. I sure as hell know I'm right.

Do I think their telling me this would have created a different outcome? Of course not. It never mattered one way or another. In the end, this was always going to happen because Joel wasn't going to listen to anyone.

"What can you tell us about Stella?" Deputy Winslow asks me. He's sitting behind his desk with a pen and paper.

"You're asking me to give you a reason to blame Stella's murder on my husband," I say.

Deputy Winslow considers me for a moment. "I think he's done enough of that since we caught him burying her body. The question is, do you want to do what is right or not?"

I sigh. They're absolutely right. Joel is in the thick of it at this point. So I might as well tell them what they want to know.

As much as I can, of course.

"Okay," I say. "But I can't go into much detail. There's still doctor and patient confidentiality." I will not break that code, even after death. Still, there are some things I can tell them.

Deputy Winslow doesn't seem too happy with that answer. I get the idea he thinks I'm some city woman who doesn't know how the world really works, when in actuality, I know more about how it works than he does. And it's not just because he lives in this small town.

"Then what can you tell me?" he asks.

"I can tell you that my husband has seemed different for a little while," I say. "For a couple of months, he hasn't totally connected with me. And then the last month, he's been having a lot of what I thought were work meetings. He told me he was traveling this weekend for work."

"And you didn't think that was odd?" Deputy Winslow asks.

"Oh, I definitely did. The thought crossed my mind that he was cheating on me," I say. "I wasn't happy about it, but I also wasn't all that happy with Joel. But honestly, it wasn't that, though. I just didn't think my own husband would start breaking the way he did."

"You really think someone can be that delusional?" Deputy Winslow asks. "I honestly never thought that kind of mental breakdown thing was real. Just for the movies."

I try not to take offense to that. "It's what my whole job is based on," I say. "So yes, it is absolutely possible."

"What about Stella?" he asks. "What are you able to say without breaking that whole doctor-patient thing?"

"I can tell you that she said she was feeling uncomfortable with someone lately," I say, trying to toe the line on what I can get away with. "That a man was following her, showing her attention she didn't like. She never told me his name, of course, but she made clear that she didn't really know him. He was just someone she met."

"And what did you tell her to do about that?"

"I told her that if he wasn't taking no for an answer and she felt unsafe, she should call the police," I say.

"Did she?"

I shrug. "If she had, she never told me. Sometimes, women in those positions explain it away and try not to jump to conclusions."

The deputy switches gears after he finishes jotting down a note. "And how often did she see you? And why down in the valley if she lives up here? Was there a specific reason she was seeing you?"

I frown. Some of those answers, I can't reveal. "You live up here full-time, right?" I ask.

He nods without saying a word.

"Then I'm sure you know who she is. The way she put it, a lot of people know each other. And since you're law enforcement, you've had a run-in with her before."

He takes a deep breath. "The accident," he says, nodding.

"Something like that can mess with someone. And even more so is the fact that not everyone liked how it came out. Is that correct?" I'm asking the questions now, trying to spin it so that he reaches the conclusion without me having to say it.

"I suppose so," he says. "There's a feeling around here that they weren't so happy together. That when she got in the car accident with her boyfriend, it was less of an accident and more about her snapping. I don't take much stock in that rumor, though."

"That's fair," I say. "But other people around town might be more hostile about those rumors."

He nods. "Those who were close to Aaron, her boyfriend, might not be so friendly to her."

"So she stayed in the valley, away from here, for a long time. But she must have wanted to get back home after all the work we've done. Or had done," I correct myself. "There was a lot of guilt she was carrying, and it was tough for her to face it up here."

The deputy sighs. I haven't given him much, but it's enough. Joel made his bed, so even if I hadn't told them anything specific, there is no way he's getting out of this one.

"Can I see my husband before you take him away?" I ask.

Deputy Winslow shrugs and motions for Deputy Larson to lead me to Joel's cell.

FORTY-FIVE

Joel

I don't know how long I've been staring at this spot on the wall, but I have been ever since they sat me down. I don't focus on anything else. I'm basically staring right through it, trying to piece together what happened to me. What happened to Stella.

The door opens. I expect to see one of the deputies, but when I lift my head, Emily is standing before me. Instead of a room to be questioned in, I'm in a jail cell. And she's on the other side of the bars.

"Hey," she says softly. The deputies let her come in alone, which is nice. I'm sure I'm not a flight risk, considering I'm locked up. And there's no way I would hurt her even if she came close to the bars. After everything, I realize how much I've wronged her.

I've wronged so many people.

"I don't know what happened," I finally say, sobbing,

snot trailing out of my nostrils. I wipe my nose on my sleeve, not caring how I look right now. "I swear, I was dating her. I mean...I don't know what I mean."

"It's okay, Joel," Emily says.

"I met her outside your office, but I had no idea she was your patient," I say. "Definitely wouldn't have done anything if I'd known she was. I'm sorry, I know that doesn't make it any better. But after that, I swear, we kept seeing each other." I pause, remembering everything over the weekend. "But I guess that wasn't reality? That I made it all up?"

I'm asking because it feels like I need someone to tell me. I can't trust my own brain anymore.

"I just broke?" I add.

Emily nods. I know it must suck to hear her husband thought he was cheating on her, but in reality, he lost his mind and was having a fake affair. Despite that it was never real, it probably still doesn't do much for her self-esteem that her husband thought he was cheating on her.

"I'm so sorry," I say. I really mean it, too. Emily has stuck with me this whole time. She could have easily told me to go to hell, spun on her heels, and walked right out of here. The fact that she hasn't tells me a lot, and I know I don't deserve her. "I've done so much to you."

"Like Angela," she says.

I freeze. I never thought I'd hear her say that name to me. I clear my throat, unsure if I'm buying time to think about what to say.

"You know about her?" I ask. With everything that has happened this weekend, I was beginning to wonder if *that* was even real. But Emily just confirmed it was.

"Joel, I know you better than you think," she says.

I'm crying again. I don't want her pity, but I'm once

more aghast at how she never decided to leave me. "You're right, and I've been awful. I never appreciated you. I'm so sorry," I say between sobs. "I guess now I'm getting what I deserve, aren't I? For what I did to you. For what happened to Angela."

"You didn't mean for Angela to die like that," she says. "You couldn't have known she would do that."

"The police didn't think so at first," I say, reliving it. "They grilled me."

"And you kept it a secret from me," she says.

I nod slowly. "I did everything I could to keep it from you. I want to say I did it to keep you from being hurt, but it was to keep me from getting caught," I admit. "Eventually, they ruled it a suicide."

"Again, you couldn't know she would."

She's right, but it doesn't change that it still happened. "But I still led her to that conclusion. If I'd never gotten involved with her, it wouldn't have happened."

"You're right about that," she says, not sugar-coating anything for me right now, which is fine. I need the tough love.

"And now Stella. That poor girl," I say, thinking about how her face looked covered in dirt. Her dead stare. "I don't know how I could do that to someone."

"It's okay," Emily says. "You didn't."

I look at her, furrowing my brows. "What do you mean?"

"You weren't in your right mind," she says. "I know that's not who you are, Joel. Truly."

My lip quivers. I can't handle it anymore. I want to wrap my arms around my wife, embrace her, but these bars keep us separated. "Thank you for believing in me," I say.

Emily smiles, and I see something behind her eyes. Like

acceptance. Like she is willing to work with me. And if she is, then I'll work with her, too. "I'm glad you're owning up to everything now."

"I just wish I didn't let it get this far," I say.

Her eyes are filled with sympathy. "So do I."

FORTY-SIX

Emily

Coming back to the office after leaving Joel at the station yesterday is kind of surreal. After all that, I can't believe I'm here. Just heading back to work like the weekend didn't change everything.

But at the same time, it feels right. Full circle, if you will.

I stand in the courtyard of the offices just before heading down the hallway to my office. I stare at a table and bench, the very one where Joel met Stella.

Joel wasn't wrong, after all. He did meet Stella here. And that's where the story splinters.

I can remember it like it was yesterday. The girl walked into my office for her first appointment. She seemed a little reserved, like she wasn't keen on sharing things. But I knew I could get her to open up.

I just didn't know what she was going to tell me.

I sat in my chair, and she sat across from me on the couch in the dimly lit room. She had a bottle of water that she set on a coaster on the table in front of her. She was very pretty, much younger than me, with a sling over her shoulder that cradled her arm.

I learned it was due to a car accident. The one that left her boyfriend dead, and her with a broken collarbone and a court-ordered mandate to see a therapist.

I don't think she would have come to see me without that mandate. She said she spent some time in the hospital, though they weren't sure she was of sound mind to keep her driver's license because of the ordeal. So, it became my job to give her the okay and clear her so that she could continue to drive. And, I think, so she could prove to everyone in town that she wasn't crazy.

Over the coming weeks, she described the car accident. How she'd slammed into a tree, was in shock, maybe even out of sorts, and that people found them.

He wasn't wearing a seatbelt, which all of his friends insisted was not like him. That he never would have taken that risk. He was all about safety.

But clearly, this time was different.

I wondered why it was different, and the more we talked, the more Stella revealed things. That he was cheating on her. That she was breaking up with him. That their happy little relationship wasn't so happy.

And then, there came a small inconsistency in her story. Nothing major—in fact, I can't remember it specifically. But it caused me to prod and pull at the threads of her story, trying to milk more and more out of her. That's what I do, after all. I get people to open up, face their demons, come to terms with their past decisions, and decide how to move forward.

And the decision she needed to move on from was a doozy.

She admitted to me that her boyfriend *had been* wearing a seatbelt. That she hadn't lost control of the car. But rather, she'd driven into that tree on purpose. And had made sure to unclip her boyfriend's seatbelt before slamming into it.

She hadn't known it would kill him, but figured the likelihood was high. Worst case—her words, not mine—he would be ejected, break a lot of bones, and learn his lesson.

That shy girl who walked into my office was no longer there. She was smug and happy about her work. All those people who knew Aaron, her boyfriend, were mad at her, and she was court-ordered to come here, yes. But there was no evidence that she had done anything to intentionally harm him.

I sat there staring at her, watching her show me her true self. It was kind of frightening. That someone could lie so well and fool even a trained professional like me.

"But you can't say anything because of doctor-patient confidentiality," she said smugly, acting like she knew more than me. She certainly had stones, but she was too arrogant. And she didn't do her research.

"You just admitted to murder in my office," I said.

She shrugged.

"I can absolutely tell the authorities. Because if I think you're at risk of doing it again, then I have an obligation to do so."

"But I'm not," she said, her eyes darting around frantically. She was caught, and she knew it. She shouldn't have been so cocky. And that's where she messed up.

"My professional opinion goes a long way," I said.

"So what, you're just going to call them now? Why even tell me this? I can run."

I thought back to the email I received from Angela. The one that laid out how she wanted Joel, but that he had chosen me. That Joel wasn't going to pay for what he had done to her.

"Because I need your help," I said.

And the rest is history.

I mean, for the most part.

Wife invites idiot husband to lunch. Cute girl needs help from idiot husband on his way to that lunch. Cute girl flirts with idiot husband. Idiot husband doesn't realize the cute girl is way out of his league because his penis removes all logic from him.

Not that he had a ton of that to begin with.

I watched the whole thing from the window.

But that was just the beginning of my plan.

FORTY-SEVEN

The weekend was the harder part. Sure, I followed Joel up there. But it wasn't just because of the rewards phone number he used. No, that was just the cherry on top. It was because I knew exactly where they were headed.

Stella and I figured it was best to use her place. Of course, we staged the cabin to look like a rental. We pulled her pictures down and the other things that made it feel homey. It helped immensely that Joel didn't want to take care of booking any of it and just gave Stella the cash.

How thoughtful of him to use our money on his new girlfriend.

But it wasn't the drive up there, seeing them together, or even hatching a plan that was so difficult.

The worst part was playing dead for so long in the backyard.

I watched as Stella shoved the air conditioner, and I let it fall to the ground. Then I had to lay down next to it, quickly apply the blood makeup to my head, and be still.

Stella, being a travel nurse—or rather, telling Joel she was one—really sold it. I figured worst case was if he didn't buy I was dead, I'd give him a scare for a moment and then yell at him for cheating on me. Not the end-all-be-all, but still something.

Luckily, he bought it. Joel isn't the best with details, as I know.

The most touching part was that Joel didn't want to touch me. He really does love me. He couldn't stomach seeing me dead or touching my lifeless corpse, so wrapping my body up in the tarp was much easier to sell with Stella handling it.

And then, of course, the hardware store being closed threw a kink in the plan. But Joel managed to get himself in more trouble by getting beat up. I wasn't there to see it, but that night, after Stella drugged his tea, she told me all about it.

That's when we made the tarp look like it had a body inside so that I didn't have to stick around inside all day while they dug the grave. I can't believe that worked, either, but again, Joel saw what he wanted to see.

Like I witnessed in my office, Stella could sell a lie to anyone. So there was no question in my mind that Joel didn't stand a chance.

There were so many hiccups, too. Like the stupid dog that chased him, or that young deputy showing up to check on things. That guy almost ruined everything, but Stella sold it to him, too.

And in the end, it all worked out, didn't it? For me, for Joel, for Stella.

Well, it worked out like I planned for Stella.

That was the part of the plan I never filled her in on.

WHILE JOEL WAS TRYING to get away from the dog, and then drove himself into a ditch because we had drugged his alcohol, we enacted the rest of the plan. While he slept, we loaded everything into his car. His luggage, clothes, and anything else he might have brought so that it looked like he was never staying there.

We put all of Stella's things back inside the cabin, which was easy enough.

But then we had to wait for Joel to get arrested by the police after Stella cried her eyes out on the phone, giving them a line of BS so that they thought Joel was crazy.

Once they were gone, we took care of the tedious task of digging the grave back up that we had filled in while he was busy in the neighbor's house.

Of course, this is the part of the plan that Stella didn't seem to understand.

"Why are we digging this back up now?" she asked. She did as she was told, though, because I had the information to sink her. But she just couldn't help but wonder.

"Because this is going to make him look even more crazy," I explained. "He'll come back and think it was filled in the night before, so it makes no sense."

"And then the deputies can corroborate that I had dug up the septic tank," she said, thinking she knew what she was talking about.

I just nodded, going with it. "You got it."

She sighed. "It just sucks because I've been digging this stupid thing all weekend," she complained.

We kept digging until the hole was fully back to what it was before. A giant pit in the middle of the yard.

"So after this, what then?" Stella asked. "Joel already looks crazy and is busted with breaking and entering. What more than stalking is there?"

I nodded, taking a few breaths, acting like I was thinking of an answer. In truth, I couldn't tell her, so I deflected.

"So what happened at the hardware store?" I asked. I had followed them around ever since I was no longer wrapped up in the tarp. I figured I might get a laugh at Joel getting into some shenanigans, but instead, I witnessed the interaction with Stella. "Some guy was pretty angry with you about something."

She sighed. "Don't worry. I told Joel it was just some dude who wouldn't take no for an answer, but he was friends with my ex. He thinks I did it on purpose. The accident, I mean. That I told Aaron not to buckle up or something and ran straight into a tree."

"But you did do that," I pointed out.

She shrugged. "He doesn't know that, though. So, what next? You think Joel's going to stop being a cheater after this?"

She was already on to the next. No remorse for anything she'd done. I saw it then, and I see it now.

"I think so," I said. "It's going to be a big mental trip for him. But there's still one more part you need to do for me."

She rolled her eyes. "Fine. What is it?"

"Die."

I took the shovel in my hands and swung it right against the side of her head. She never saw it coming and took the blow full force. She fell backward, straight into the hole we had just dug. She crumpled like someone who was still alive would never do, the blood from the back of her head already seeping into the dirt.

I groaned as I took the first shovel full of dirt and threw it on top of her lifeless body.

"You were right. All this digging does suck," I said to her

corpse. I continued on until the hole was back to being fully covered.

And then my phone rang. The sheriff's department, right on time. Officer Winslow told me I needed to come pick up my husband because he'd been arrested. Of course, I would need some time to get there, when in reality, I needed time to cover up the body.

And then came the night he refused to confess to me in the hotel. I knew Joel would have enough time to dig up the grave again, so I gave that time to him the night he left me alone in the hotel and didn't call the police until morning. I figured he would have gotten far enough, and once again, I was right.

The plan seemed preposterous when I came up with it, but somehow, to my astonishment, it all worked out exactly right. I can't help but feel a little proud of myself.

Joel never deserved to die for what he did. He wasn't a killer. He couldn't have known that Angela was going to commit suicide. He was just an asshole.

He deserved to pay, yes. But not die.

Stella is the one who deserved to die. She's the one who killed her boyfriend and had no remorse.

And now it's all finished. The plan came together and even with the few mishaps along the way, there isn't a single loose thread exposed that I can think of.

EPILOGUE

Deputy Larson walked into the station and slid into his seat next to Deputy Winslow. It had been a slow week after catching Joel Rosenthal, but it was a welcome slowness after all that had transpired. Deputy Winslow had far more experience than Deputy Larson, and even he was shocked at how that case had ended.

Rosenthal was transferred to county lockup a couple of days after he was arrested, and all was back to normal.

But now Deputy Larson had a question that he needed to figure out.

"Hey, you remember Rosenthal's car at the impound?" Deputy Larson asked Deputy Winslow.

Deputy Winslow shrugged. "I guess so. What about it?"

"Well, I had to move it so that Chuck could bring the tow truck through, but I got curious and looked in the glove box," he said. "I found this DVR box inside of it."

"Wasn't Marlon saying someone broke into his cabin and stole one of those from his house?" Deputy Winslow asked. "We thought he was crazy, 'cause why would anyone steal just that?"

Deputy Larson nodded. "I think so. Hate to have to apologize to that guy."

Another shrug from Deputy Winslow. "Maybe we should plug it in and see what's on it."

Deputy Larson made quick work of the cables at Deputy Winslow's desk and fired it up. He found the icons, started clicking through them, and got to the one labeled with last Friday's date.

And then he hit play.

For a special deleted scene from Stella's point-of-view, you can find it here:
https://BookHip.com/DMZLCTC

LAST MINUTE GUEST

He wanted to step out of his comfort zone, but stumbled into a nightmare.

One year after his sister's death, **Edward** decides to follow through with their dream of opening their guesthouse as a vacation rental.

At first, **Jax** seems like the ideal guest. He's everything Edward wishes he could be. Handsome, outgoing, and not a care in the world.

But as the days pass, things don't seem to be going as well as Edward expected. Jax is inserting himself into Edward's life, conveniently bumping into him at his work, and then there are the dates he brings back to the guesthouse.

The dates Edward never sees leave...

Edward realizes that he has no idea who the man is that is renting his guesthouse. But the question remains, is he prepared to find out?

Last Minute Guest: A suspenseful psychological thriller with a jaw-dropping twist

AFTERWORD

Thanks for reading A Secret Worth Keeping!

Fun fact, my wife and I used to own a cabin that we rented out. Did events from that experience end up in this book? Yes. Is the whole book a true story? What a crazy coincidence that would be. Haha.

This story was a bit more "out there" than I'm used to writing, but it was a lot of fun to piece it all together.

I have to thank my wife, Sara, for always being a sounding board for my stories. For letting me whine when I couldn't figure out some connections, for offering insight that I can't see, and for always supporting me. I love you, honey!

Thanks to my author friends Sonja Sargent and Douglas Pratt for telling me to keep going when I was struggling to put pieces together.

Thanks to Tony Strong for making such an awesome cover for me.

Thanks to my editor Chelsey Heller and proofreader Lisa Lee. It's amazing what manages to slip through!

And, of course, thanks to all my readers for picking up this book and allowing me to continue writing!

As always, being an independent author, I don't have a huge publisher's budget, so reviews are very important. If you have the time, please consider popping over to Amazon, or your favorite place to leave reviews, and post one!

- Drew Strickland

March 16, 2024

ALSO BY DREW STRICKLAND

Flesh of the Sons (Book 2)

Valley of Dying Stars (Book 3)

The Soulless Wanderers Series

Tribulation (Book 0)

Soulless Wanderers (Book 1)

Patriarch (Book 2)

Exodus (Book 3)

Resurrection (Book 4)

Coming Soon! (Book 5)

ABOUT THE AUTHOR

Drew Strickland is the author of the Sheriff Elven Hallie Mystery series, Soulless Wanderers: a post-apocalyptic zombie thriller series, and the co-author of the Carolina McKay thriller series and the Cannibal Country series, both written with Tony Urban. When he isn't writing, he enjoys reading, watching horror movies and spending time with his wife and children.

www.drewstricklandbooks.com